Francis Bede writes and lives in Tasmania

Bede, Francis
God in the Human Machine – a theobiography
ISBN: 978-0-9806289-2-0
Copyright © 2021 Francis Bede
First edition.

God in the Human Machine – a theobiography

By Francis Bede

Introduction

When the child Frank is raised in the ordinariness of suburbia with the expectation of achieving the highest position on earth, that of a Catholic priest, it is theology, in the words and ecclesiology of the Church, which sanctifies his purpose. When he accomplishes this elevation through his unique spiritual energy, having been called by God and guided by the Church, Frank will be placed at the head of the world as a shining light, upon whom the aged may look with gladness, the young with inspiration, and the suffering with hope.

The intense theological life of Frank O'Connor, his rise before, and his test during his time in the seminary, is not only an example of the Catholic genius for elevating a life from ordinary circumstances; it is also an examination of the Catholic Church's vision for its priests. The manifest object of the Church on Earth is to exercise its Divine authority over humanity through its priest agents such as Frank, and thus be an inspired presence in the World, a force truthfully mandated by the Christ himself.

Frank as priest will be required to feel intensely his conviction, and to understand and love the supernatural logic of Catholic theology. Frank must prove that his God given role is first before all else that is demanded for him. In the teeth of volatile life chances, he must prove himself equal to those who oppose him. Having been born into the threshold world of the priesthood an opportunity has been presented to Frank to rise above the ordinary and prove his worth, with learning and eloquence, with only his faith to give him strength.

The story of Frank's calling to the priesthood begins for the reader at a time in Frank's early childhood, when, as a shy sensitive child, who was beginning to realise there were many things he could not yet explain to himself, he began peering into and poking about the layers of right and

1

wrong, of delight and of wonder, of questions and answers. The promise of all things which Catholicism offers to all the young like Frank is the first step on the spiritual pathway to Catholic immortality.

Through his Catholic education Frank will develop a keen interest in daily human life. An original breadth of Catholic sense will build for him a way to see, weigh, and compare whatever passes before him, kindling a desire to search out and define the mysterious relationships of things not so clear, and which are uniquely associated with the marvellous and the supernatural. He will develop a sacred thirst for saving souls and for learning, first as a means of attaining altruistic authority, then as a most desirable end in itself. His Holy Spirit's inspiration will become an unfaltering energy, a determination to obtain what his soul pronounces as immutable; a majestic priesthood, determined courage, a deep and agonizing sympathy for the meek and the weak, empathy for such crushed humanity as bled by all kinds of despotism, and an extraordinary depth of passion, together with that rare alliance between faith and passion, which enables the former, when deeply roused, to excite, develop and sustain the latter.

This state of enthusiasm for the teachings of the Catholic Church will then carry Frank forward on a momentum he was only too happy to join. Everybody who knew him wanted it. Nothing else mattered; neither family, sexual love, nor a paying job. He was becoming less ordinary; and upon entering the seminary, and after six years he will become extraordinary. The eloquence of his faith will be boundless, his conviction decisive. And he need never look far for spiritual, emotional and financial support should he ever stumble. The Church is there for him. He need only willingly and without question follow its directions and God will do the rest. He is to join a special fraternity, a family of brethren like no other. These men are exclusive brothers in the Christ, who have been chosen by their God to work tirelessly for the world. And in imitation of the Christ they will save the world.

It is God alone to whom Frank will articulate his most private thoughts. When his doubts become a crisis, he will ask God to give him a sign, a personal sign that he has indeed been rightly chosen, and that God has good works planned for him, for God does not err in His judgments of His people. But there is also another voice. It is the voice of his conscience. The Devil has not changed since the Garden of Eden. It whispers a sweet tune in Frank's ear. Are you really free, he will ask. There are women beyond the seminary walls who will love him. He will have children who will adore him. He will have a job which fulfils him. He will have fun. There is a real life out there. The times, they are always a-changing. He will not be an instrument like he is in the seminary. There is no love like unconditional love. The Church says it loves him, but there are conditions: celibacy, orthodoxy and dogma, for him to strictly follow to earn that love.

And should his yearning for the love of a woman become an overwhelming feeling he fears he cannot overcome, the Virgin Mary, the holiest of women, pure, undefiled, sweet and innocent, will be there for him. He is free to love her and to yearn for her. She will help him get his rest at night. His priestly virginity and her immaculate virginity are forever wed in the sanctity of faith, hope and charity. She is the most beautiful woman who has ever lived. She is the ideal woman for a Catholic priest because he is free at any time and in any place to emotionally reach for her. Her body is unimportant. And it is only through prayer that she will respond. Her mystery is that which awaits Frank to discover. Then he will have peace. Yet the Devil will sit with him while he prays to her. He will describe her body, he will describe her sensual touch, and he will describe her sexual yearning for him, and his for her. The Devil will describe to Frank the pleasures of auto eroticism which he will arouse when Frank yearns for the Virgin Mary.

But Frank must resist, resist, else he will eventually pervert his calling and become as the Devil wishes him to be, a corrupted idealistic priest who had once risen to the gates of Heaven; and being especially perverted, falling, he won't land until he reaches the fiery pits of Hell. And the Devil is cunning, for should Frank fall he need not actually leave the priesthood. He can be a corrupt priest and his God will still love and forgive him, as long as he is loyal to his Church and perform his duties to the Church's satisfaction. Together they are safely the fraternity of the silent whose secrets are not for the world to see. The Devil will tell him the Church needs him more than ever. There are fewer men who feel selfless enough to answer God's needful calling. Frank will have his security; and the Catholic Church its. The Devil will tell Frank that even though there have been centuries of Catholic Church scandal God has always resisted them. For the Church has been chosen by God to prevail until the final judgment.

But there is another way for Frank should he become like Prometheus, and that is unbelief, over which neither a God nor a Devil has any power. Unbelief grants him the strength to walk away from his Church. Either from anger or by self-preservation, Frank might feel that the Church has no real power over anyone. And should Frank exercise his free will and decide not to believe, then he must therefore leave the culture of the priesthood and of the Church. Only for apostate believers is the Devil more real than God. And whoever is not with God is against God; and whoever does not gather with God must scatter in the world and live as loner unbelievers.

The questions and answers of faith and belief are Frank's living dilemma. They are long and seemingly endless: his fantastical tale now to be told from this page on.

4

Part 1

The theological rise of Frank O'Connor

Canon 1 - His history before Frank was born

The Angel's Chorus:
IN THE SUPERNATURAL FRANK IS BORN,
OUR THREE-WAY GOD IS FOR HIM TO WORSHIP,
A GRACIOUS CHURCH WAS BUILT TO WARN,
FOR IN EVERY BREATH IS THE URGE TO SIN.

The implicit nature of God, that of his goodness and love, is revealed to the human world through his Son, the Christ, through his deeds and words, who, in Catholic theological history, came to Earth specifically to save humanity by sacrificing his life for them. And Frank when he is born, by the grace of the Holy Spirit, who is also God, is to share in the divine life of the saviour the Christ, so that he too can be saved.

Catholic theological history tells that conscious human life began when God created Frank's first parents, Adam and Eve, inviting them to enter an intimate communion with him. This intimacy didn't last, because they disobeyed him, and they fell down in disgrace. They and their descendants lost their nakedness to clothing, they had to work, they suffered pain and illness; they would die. However, God was not entirely displeased with them. In loving forgiveness for when humans have learnt to atone for their sins, God would continue his revelations to them, and promise salvation for all who fear and are subservient to him. (For it is written that the gender of authority is male).

God's revelations were accomplished through his Word made flesh in the form of the Christ. Thus, what the Christ said God said. The Christ, being the only-begotten Son of God who became the incarnate man, was the perfect and definitive Word of the Father. And in the sending of the Son and the gift of the Spirit, the revelation that is God's word was complete in the Christ. It is written that in giving to humanity his Son, God gave all that was needed, for there was nothing else to give. What the Christ said truly mattered, as revealed by God's earthly authority, the Church, through what came to be known as the Catholic tradition.

The first Evangelicals entrusted the deposit of faith to the whole of the Church, which the Christ had said is his rock. And thanks to a supernatural sense of faith, the people of God, assisted by the Holy Spirit and guided by the Magisterium of the Church, never ceases to welcome the fallen, to penetrate life in all flesh ever more deeply and to live more fully through the gift of divine revelation. And though the people of God see themselves as imperfect, the Church, as the one and true beacon of hope, deems itself to be nothing less than perfect, in other words infallible. Any wrong the Church has done, cannot be spiritually wrong, because the Christ has said so himself.

The task of providing the true interpretation of the living faith is entrusted to the teaching authority of the Church alone. For the Pope is the successor of the apostle Peter, the first Bishop of Rome, and of all teachers in communion with him. To this Magisterium is given the gift of telling the truth in the service of the Word of God, and to which is also given the task of defining human behaviour formulated directly from the truth contained in divine Revelation. Scripture, Tradition, and the Church Magisterium are so closely linked with each other that neither of them can stand without the other. Working together, each in its own way, under the action of the one Holy Spirit, they all contribute effectively to the salvation of souls.

Sacred Scripture must only be read and interpreted under the full guidance of the Magisterium of the Church, and according to three criteria. The first, it must be read with keen attention to the content and unity of the whole of Scripture. The second, it must be read within the living tradition of the Church. The third, it must be read with attention given to the inner harmony which exists within the truth of faith itself. It gives support and generates vigour in the life of the Church. For the children of the Church, it is a confirmation of the faith, food for the soul and the fount of a spiritual life. Sacred Scripture is the soul of theology and of pastoral preaching.

The symbols of faith are the professions of creeds composed by the Church from its very beginning, to be set forth systematically in a normal language common to all the faithful. It begins with the baptismal creed because Baptism is conferred in the name of the Father, and of the Son, and of the Holy Spirit, and the truths of faith professed at Baptism are articulated in reference to the three Persons of the Most Holy Trinity. The Profession of Faith must begin with 'I believe in God' because this affirmation is the most important, being the source of all the other truths about the future Frank and about the world, and about the entire life of all like Frank who will be born to believe in God.

In revealing his name, God makes known the riches contained in the fabulous mystery of his being. He alone is from everlasting to everlasting. He is the One who transcends the world and history. It is he who made heaven and earth. He is the highest holiness, always ready to forgive. He is the One who is spiritual, transcendent, omnipotent, eternal, personal, and perfect. He is truth and love. God is truth itself and as such he can neither deceive nor be deceived. He is light, and in him there is no darkness. It is said that when God revealed himself to Israel as the One, he also revealed that he has a stronger love than that of parents for their children or of husbands and wives for their spouses. God as himself is love, who gives himself completely and gratuitously, who so loves the world that he gave his only Son for the world to be saved through his death and resurrection. By sending his Son, the Christ, and through the Holy Spirit, God reveals that he himself is eternal love.

God has left some traces of his Trinitarian being in creation and in the Old Testament but his inmost being as the Holy Trinity is a mystery accessible only to the reasoning of the Catholic Church. The Christ, through the Church, will reveal to Frank that God is 'Father', not only insofar as he created the universe and the mankind, but above all because he eternally generated in his bosom the Son who is his Word - the radiance of the glory of God. The Church expresses her Trinitarian faith by professing a belief in the oneness of God in whom there are three Persons: Father, Son, and Holy Spirit. The three divine Persons are one God because each of them equally possesses the fullness of the one and indivisible divine nature. They are truly distinct from each other by reason of the relations which place them in correspondence to each other. The Father generates the Son; the Son is generated by the Father; the Holy Spirit proceeds from the Father and the Son. Inseparable in their one substance, the three divine Persons are also inseparable in their activity. The Trinity has one operation, sole and the same. In this one divine action, however, each Person is present according to the mode which is proper to him in the Trinity.

Canon 2 - The theological coming of Frank into the world

The Angel's Chorus:
BY THE WATERS OF BAPTISM HE WILL BE KNOWN,
IT'S A TRADITION SINCE THE FIRST WATERS RAN,
INTO AN IMMERSED LIFE FRANK IS THROWN,
SAVED AT BIRTH SO HE MAY PEACEFULLY DIE.

Soon after his birth in 1945 Frank was baptised and immersed into the death of the Christ to then rise with him as a new creature. This sacrament is also called the bath of regeneration and renewal in the Holy Spirit and it is also called enlightenment because the baptized Frank becomes a son of light. Baptism is pre-empted in various ways: water, seen as source of life and of death; in the Ark of Noah, which was saved by means of water; in the passing through the Red Sea, which liberated Israel from Egyptian slavery; in the crossing of the Jordan River, which brought Israel into the Promised Land, showing the way to eternal life. At the beginning of his public life the Christ was himself baptized by John the Baptist in the Jordan. On the cross, blood and water, signs of Baptism and the Eucharist, flowed from his pierced side. After his Resurrection he gave to his apostles this mission to go forth and make disciples of all nations, baptizing them in the name of the Father and of the Son and of the Holy Spirit. And from the day of Pentecost, the Church has administered Baptism to all who believe in the Christ as the Son of God.

The essential rite of this sacrament consisted of immersing Frank in water or pouring water over his head while invoking the name of the Father and the Son and the Holy Spirit. Because Frank was not yet baptised, he was able to receive Baptism. The Church baptizes infants like Frank because they are born with original sin. They need to be freed from the power of the Evil One and brought into the realm of freedom which belongs to the children of God. When Frank the infant was baptized, he was required to make a profession of faith. This is done by his parents and by the Church.

The Baptismal rite removed original sin from the infant Frank, but not his personal sins to come. For them Frank is given the state of grace after he has revealed them to the mysteriously angelic priest at the sacrament of Confession. A baptized Frank belongs forever to the Christ. His name is marked with the indelible seal of the character of the Christ.

Frank's name, Francis at Baptism, was important because God knows him by that name, that is, in his uniqueness as a person. In Baptism a Catholic receives his or her own name in the Church. It should preferably be the name of a saint who can best offer the baptized a model of sanctity and an assurance of his or her intercession before God when life's difficulties emerge.

Canon 3 - The Catholic Educating of young Frank

The Angel's Chorus:
HE'LL LEARN ABOUT US AND DO GOD'S WILL,
HE HAS A SOUL FOR WHICH HE MUST CARE FOR,
HAVING A GUARDIAN ANGEL GIVES HIM A THRILL,
BIBLICAL STORIES 'LL TEACH HIM WHAT TO FEEL.

Frank's parents, when they brought Frank into the world, knew that it was going to be a struggle raising him in the Catholic faith. Christian Catholics have been persecuted since the earliest times. It was therefore his parents' duty to arm Frank with a joyous outlook so he might live the Catholic life aware that it would pose problems for him. The threatening world will mock and question his Catholicism, his desire to be modest, chaste, kind, generous, charitable, good and holy. The diabolical outside world will tempt Frank to pursue lust, vanity, pride and covetousness. These he must reject and instead always reach for higher goals. It is from God alone with the loving support of the Church that Frank will gain perfect strength as he strives to do God's will. And his angelic young face indeed shone with a mighty sanctifying grace.

Because Frank's parents were good Catholics, they were Frank's little rock as he grew and matured to be made ready for the world. Through them he learnt modesty, kindness, self control, and love. He learnt to love the Mass and its sacraments. He said the rosary every night with them. His Catholic faith is to be entirely integrated in his life, both for his good and for the good of the world. There will be growing pains, but Frank's growth toward holiness, would be a family endeavour complemented by the Church's encouragement and assistance.

Frank's parents nightly read him passages from the Bible before he went to sleep. He got little plastic rosaries to meditate on, and on snuggling into his down pillow his imagination soared hearing the Biblical stories

12

of the sacred mysteries of God. The words of the Bible excited him greatly; greater than the fairy tales his older sister told him. He also learnt the basics of apologetics, for he must always be ready to defend the Faith. Thus, Frank further bonded with his parents. They were delighted to see in Frank the makings of a Catholic priest. He was learning how to be reliant on God's good graces, and to trust him. He found it easy and natural to rejoice in his life, and be thankful for it. God was truly good to him.

Frank learnt about angels, these purely spiritual creatures, incorporeal, invisible, immortal; beings endowed with acute intelligence and utter beauty. They ceaselessly contemplate God face-to-face and they glorify him. They serve him and are his messengers in the accomplishment of his saving mission to all. And Frank had one to guard him, St Francis, also known to him by his sister's nick-name Woo, which stands beside him as a protector and shepherd ready to help him lead a good Catholic life.

If Frank wasn't going to be called to the priesthood, he would have been predestined by God to marry a woman he would love, and together produce Catholic children in the perfect image of the invisible God. Frank is taught that man and woman were created by God in equal dignity. At the same time, they have been created to reciprocate their gender. God has willed each for the other to form a communion of persons. They are called to transmit human life by cleaving as one flesh in holy matrimony. They are likewise called to subdue the earth as stewards of God. In creating man and woman God has given them a special participation in his own divine life in holiness and justice.

Frank as human is at once corporeal and spiritual. In him spirit and matter form one nature. This unity is so profound that, thanks to the spiritual principle which is the soul, and the body which is material, Frank is a living human body who participates in the dignity of the image of God. Frank's spiritual soul did not come from his parents but from conception, when the soul is immediately created by God and is immortal. It does not perish at the moment when separated from Frank's body at death, because Frank's soul will be reunited with his body at the moment of the final resurrection.

Canon 4 - The great reason Frank was born into sin

The Angel's Chorus:
ADAM AND EVE HAD TESTED GOD'S NERVES,
BANISHED THEN WHEN THEY FELL INTO SIN,
NOW HUMANS LIVE IN THE CENTRE OF CURVES,
AND THRIVE IN THE MUNICIPALITY OF SODOM.

Sin has been present since the beginning of humanity. This reality of sin can be understood clearly only in the light of divine revelation and above all in the light of the Christ the Saviour of all. Where sin abounds, God makes grace to abound all the more. When tempted by the Devil, the first man and woman allowed trust in their Creator to die in their hearts. In their disobedience they wished to become like God and be independent, but it was not in accordance with God wishes.

From the very beginning humanity has held a special place in God's creation. Composed of both flesh and spirit, humans were created in the divine image of the soul and were imbued with original holiness, justice and freewill. God placed humankind with the dominion over the fish of the sea, the birds of the air, and all the living things that move on the earth. Along with the gift of a soul came the gift of free will. God, desiring the free love of mankind and viewing them as his children rather than slaves and servants, gave Adam and Eve the free will to accept or reject God's love. Before their temptation at the hands of the Devil, Adam and Eve chose to accept and return the love of their Creator, and submit to obedience out of love for God. In this self-dominion and equilibrium, they lived a happy life for they were pure and well ordered in all their being because they were free from the rebellious need to succumb to the pleasures of the senses, to covet earthly goods and the need to assert themselves against the dictates of God's divine reason. There was order in their relationship with each other, in the communion and intimacy that makes for joy and happiness, and they were naked, but they were not ashamed.

Then the dark and seductive voice of the Devil entered into their realm. Out of hatred for God it sought their ruin. Church tradition and teachings implore that evil could not originate from God, the source of justice and quintessence of holiness. Evil itself, the rejection of the loving grace of God, began with the angel Lucifer. God created Lucifer as a good angel, a being of pure spirit. Lucifer as a spiritual creature was one of beauty, power and intelligence. Like all creatures Lucifer was created to love God and serve him, but Lucifer began to focus on his own individual power, intelligence and qualities. Rather than attribute his strengths and qualities to the service and love of his creator, Lucifer turned from God and sought himself as the source of his own pleasures and service. He was responsible for himself alone. By a free choice, Lucifer rejected God and he was thrown out of Heaven. He took with him many other angels, who likewise rejected God. By separating themselves from the creator, the fallen angels introduced evil into creation and authored the first sin. The fallen angels' sin could not be forgiven because it is the irrevocable character of their choice, and not a defect of the infinite divine mercy. There was no repentance for the angels after their fall, just as there is no repentance for humans who seek it without the divine help of Catholic priests.

God had warned Adam from the beginning that he was free to eat from any of the trees of the garden except the tree of knowledge of good and evil. From that tree he shall not eat. The moment he eats from it he is doomed to die. The Garden of Eden contained two special trees. The first was the forbidden tree of knowledge of good and evil and the second tree was the tree of everlasting life. This Genesis story, Frank's favourite, tells of Adam and Eve disobeying God's commandment and falling into sin. They freely chose to defy God by eating from the forbidden tree of good and evil. The Church teaches that this first sin by a human constituted a loss of trust in God and an abuse of the freedom of mankind.

Because they had disobeyed their creator and indulged in sin, Adam and Eve instantly knew of evil and therefore lost God's original justice and holiness. Their privileged and harmonious state in the Garden of Evil was torn asunder and devastating results ensued. For the first time, death entered into the world and they and their descendants became doomed to live as terminal beings. For they were dirt, and to dirt they shall return. People became destined to toil and work for a living. By the sweat on their faces and dirt on their hands shall humanity forthwith get its food to eat and water to drink. Because of Eve's sin God gave women the intense pain of childbearing; in pain shall children now be brought forth. And a woman's urge shall be for her husband, and she shall have him as her master. Nature also turned against humanity. For cursed be the ground humans walk on and be the air they breathed because of their sinfulness.

The abuse of the tree of the knowledge of good and evil presents to Frank something he must recognize and respect. Frank depends on the Creator and is subject to the laws by which the Creator has established the order of the world - the essential order of existence. Frank, by his connection with Adam and Eve is also subject to the moral norms which regulate the use of freedom. The primordial test is Frank's use of his free will, and his freedom. Will Frank, by his life, confirm the fundamental order of creation and the truth that he himself is created by God, in the image of God? Will he know his limitations and repent for them?

Frank's sins do not primarily originate in his heart and conscience, nor do they arise from his spontaneous initiative. Already the Devil had placed in humanity suspicion and accusations towards God, the sole source of all that is granted to his spiritual children. Adam and Eve had claimed the power to know good and evil like God and they had chosen themselves over God. And they, by yielding to the suggestion of the Terrible Tempter, became the slaves and accomplices of God hating spirits. To have power over themselves they must permanently reject God, and be in contempt of God, and hate everything connected with God and all that comes from God. And this hatred has become the universal infection of all humanity. The Bible tells it all. In the course of its history, sin is manifested not only as an action clearly directed against God, but it is also an attempt to act independently of God as if God has never existed apart from what lies in the human mind.

Divine Revelation and the Magisterium of the Church, its only authentic interpreter, constantly and systematically speaks of the presence and universality of sin in human history. This sinful situation, repeated from generation to generation is perceptible through the phenomenon of moral sickness which is noticeable in personal and social life, and is most recognizable and striking when the Church scrutinises the human interior. Sacred Scripture impels human beings to seek the root of sin in their interior, and in their conscience and their hearts. The mysteries of the universality and hereditary nature of sin, which all humans receive from the moment of conception, should lead them on the path of the Catholic teaching on original sin. It is a case of a truth transmitted implicitly in the Church's teaching from its very beginning. The Church's teaching on original sin has been extremely valuable to Frank who, in later life, is expected as priest-in-waiting to struggle to understand the mysterious and distressing aspects of evil. His only hope is that his wavering between hasty and fleeting optimism and the urgent bouts of extreme pessimism bereft of all hope will bring him closer to God.

Fortunately for Frank, God's mercy prevails over sin and death. The passion, death and resurrection of the Christ had been offered for all of Frank's sins, so that he can be saved by the grace of God when he repents. Yet like all gifts, he must continue to choose to accept it so that he may understand his guilt. God's other gift to Frank, free will, cannot

18

be revoked. Thus, God will not force his love and grace upon Frank. He must freely choose the grace of God and offer his soul in conformity with God's will. The Christ had said through his Church that unless Frank is born again by water and by the Holy Ghost, he cannot enter into the kingdom of God. Baptism, the sacrament of faith, has cleansed Frank's soul and sanctified it with grace of the Holy Spirit. By baptism's water of rebirth, Frank's original sin is therefore forgiven and cleansed away and replaced with the grace of God. Frank's journey in the spiritual Catholic life had indeed begun.

Canon 5 - Why Frank must believe in the Christ, the Only Son of God and the Savour of the World

The Angel's Chorus:
THE GOOD NEWS CAME IN THE CHRIST'S MAN-FORM,
THE ONE WHO SORELY DIED TO SAVE HUMANITY,
THE MASTER OF FORGIVING, SO LOVING AND SO WARM,
NO-ONE CAN IGNORE SUCH A RIGHTEOUS HE.

The Good News for humanity is the proclamation of the Christ, the Son of the living God, who died and rose from the dead. In the time of King Herod and the Emperor Caesar Augustus, God fulfilled the promises that he made to Abraham and his descendants. He sent his Son, born of a virgin woman, born under the Roman law, to redeem the world. After the Christ's death and resurrection, the first disciples burned with the desire to proclaim Him in order to lead all to faith in him. From the loving knowledge of the Christ, every true believer possesses in them the powerful desire to evangelize and catechize, that is, to reveal in the person of the Christ the entire design of God and to put humanity in communion with him. The Christ in Greek means Messiah and in Hebrew the Christ means the anointed one. The Christ as man was consecrated by God and anointed by the Holy Spirit for his redeeming mission. He is the Messiah awaited by Israel, sent into the world by the Father. The Christ accepted the title of Messiah for he was the one who proclaimed himself as the one descended from Heaven, who was then crucified, who then rose from the dead; the one who gave his life in order to save all of humanity.

The Church as Magisterium confirms that the Christ is true God and true man, with two natures, a divine nature and a human nature, not confused with each other but united in the person of the Word through the Word written and spoken. Therefore, in the humanity of the Christ, all things, his miracles, his suffering, and his death, must be attributed to his divine person which acts by means of his assumed human nature.

For the young Frank these are the words he was to hear in his head in every waking moment of his day. "O Only-begotten Son and Word of God, you who are immortal, you who live for my salvation, who became incarnate of the holy Mother of God and ever Virgin Mary, conceived in her womb by the power of the Holy Spirit, not by the seed of a man. You who are one of the Holy Trinity, glorified with the Father and the Holy Spirit, save me!"

The entire life of the Christ was a revelation. What was visible in his earthly life lead believers like Frank to the invisible mystery of the Christ's divine sonship, for whoever has seen Him has seen the Father. And, even though salvation comes completely from the cross and the resurrection, the entire life of the Christ was a mystery of redemption because everything that he did and said and suffered had for its aim the salvation of every fallen human being and the restoration of their vocation as children of God.

When the Christ organised his Church, he chose twelve men, the future witnesses of his Resurrection, and made them sharers of his mission and of his authority to teach, to absolve sins, and to build up and govern the Church. In this collegiate, Peter received the keys to the Kingdom of Heaven and he assumed the first place with the mission to keep the faith in its integrity and to strengthen his brothers. Then, at the established time and when all was in place, the Christ chose to go to Jerusalem to suffer his passion and death, and to rise from the dead. As the Messiah King who showed forth the coming of the Kingdom, he humbly entered into Jerusalem mounted on a donkey.

The Christ's sacrifice began with the Last Supper, and sitting with his apostles on the eve of his passion the Christ anticipated his sacrifice, making it really present by saying "This is my Body which is given for you and this is my Blood which is poured out." Thus, he both instituted the Eucharist in memory of his sacrifice while establishing his apostles as priests of this new covenant. And despite the crucifixion horror of the Christ's death it represented the sacred humanity of the Christ, the author of Life, and the earthly will of the Son of God faithful to the heavenly will of the Father, in order that the horrible death of the Christ be for Frank's salvation.

The Christ accepted his duty to his Father; the duty of carrying Frank's future sins in his Body. Then nailed to the cross the bleeding and suffocating Christ freely offered his life as a cleansing sacrifice, that is, he made reparation for Frank's future sins with the full obedience of his love unto death. This love of the Son of God for all humanity then reconciled humanity with the Father by the Christ's death on the cross. The paschal sacrifice of the Christ redeemed humanity in a way that is unique, perfect, and definitive, opening up for humanity a communion with God through his disciples on Earth until the end of the world, when the final reckoning of body and soul will take place at the last judgment.

After the Christ's death on the cross, the power of God preserved his body from corruption and the Christ descended into Hell, a place for the billions of dead souls to dwell, both righteous and evil, who had died before the Christ. With his soul united to his divine person, the Christ went straight to the just in Hell who were patiently awaiting their Redeemer, so at last they came into the vision of God. When he had conquered by his death both death and the Devil, who has the power of death, the Christ freed the just who stood beside the Redeemer and he opened for them the gates of Heaven.

Then on the third day the Christ rose on Earth, and along with the essential sign of the empty tomb, he was proclaimed by the women who loved the Christ as risen, who then hysterically proclaimed his rising to the apostles. The Christ risen then appeared to Peter and then to the Twelve. Following that he appeared to more than five hundred of the brethren at one time and to others as well. The apostles could not have invented the story of the resurrection since it seemed impossible to them. And because it was impossible, they therefore believed. And further, the Christ had scolded them for their unbelief. And this righteous scolding, delivered by the Christ's authorised followers, has continued down to Frank's day.

For the purposes of assisting the young Frank's belief, his teachers have told him in good faith that although the Christ's death is recorded as an historical event, verifiable and attested by signs and testimonies, the Christ's Resurrection, insofar as it is the entrance of the Christ's humanity into the glory of God, transcends and surpasses history to become THE mystery of Catholic faith. For this reason, the Christ risen did not show himself to the world but to his disciples alone, making them his witnesses for the people, so that they will go forth and proclaim him. The Resurrection of the Christ was not a return to earthly life. His risen body shows that he was crucified and which bore the marks of his passion. However, the Christ's body is also of the divine life, with the characteristics of a glorified body. Because of this, the Christ risen was utterly free to appear to his disciples how and where he wished.

The Christ's Ascension into Heaven was the climax of the Christ's Incarnation. It confirmed the divinity of the Christ and all the things which he did and taught. It fulfilled all the divine promises made for Frank. Furthermore, the Christ risen, the conqueror of sin and death, procured for Frank the grace of filial adoption by God; the truest and realest share in the life of God's only begotten Son. At the end of time God will raise Frank's body from his grave. And then one day the Christ will return in glory for all Catholics who live and pray in watchful anticipation of it, for there is nothing else to live for. And the young Frank secretly hoped it would happen in his day.

All of humanity is called by the Christ to enter the Kingdom of God. Even the worst of sinners, scoffers and atheists, are called to accept the boundless mercy of the Father. Already here on earth, the Kingdom belongs to those who, with a humble heart, accept it. To them the mysteries of the Kingdom are there to be revealed. The secrets of hearts will be brought to light as well as the conduct of each one toward God and toward their neighbours. Everyone, according to how he and she has lived, will either be filled with life or damned for eternity. In this way, the fullness of the Christ will come about in which God will be all to all. Frank need not worry because he was a good boy who will grow to be a good man, a priest expectedly, doing the Christ bidding with a free will and a loving heart.

Canon 6 - Frank the altar boy and why the church is Catholic

The Angel's Chorus:
BY ALTAR SERVING FRANK IS BETTER THAN GOOD,
HOLINESS LIKE THIS IS DIFFICULT TO EARN,
ENCOURAGED BY THE CHURCH HE DOES AS HE SHOULD,
IT HELPS WITH HIS CATHOLIC REASONING WHY.

The word Church refers to the people whom God calls and gathers together from every part of the earth. They form the assembly of those who, through faith and Baptism have become children of God, members of the Christ's Body, and temples of the Holy Spirit. In Sacred Scripture there are many images which depict the mystery of the Church. The Old Testament offers images which describe the people of God. The New Testament offers images which are linked to the Christ as the Head of this people which is his Body. Images of him profess his ubiquity in human life: such images as, flocks of sheep, grapevines, rock faces, in mirrors, climactic spume, through fear; in sadness and hope, in joy and pain.

The Christ is the distal Head to the body, the Church. The Church lives from him, in him and for him. The Christ and the Church make up the whole of the sacred body in head and congregation form, one and the same mystical person, in unity for the world's salvation. The Church is called the Bride of the Christ because the Lord called himself her Spouse. The Christ has loved the Church and has joined himself to her in an everlasting covenant. He has given himself up for her in order to purify her with his blood and to sanctify her, making her the fruitful mother of all the children of God. And though the term body expresses the unity of the head with its congregation, the term bride emphasizes the distinction of the two in their personal relationship with God. The Church is also called the temple of the Spirit because the Holy Spirit resides in the body which is the Church, in her Head and in her flock.

The Holy Spirit also builds up the Church in charity by the Word of God, the sacraments, the virtues, and the offering of its divine gifts which are bestowed on individuals for the good of others, the needs of the world, and in particular for the building up of the Church. The discernment of divine gifts is the sole responsibility of the Magisterium of the Church on behalf of the Christ.

The Church is catholic in that it is universal, insofar as the Christ is ever present in her. For where there is the Christ, there is the Catholic Church. The Church proclaims the fullness and the totality of the faith. She as bride bears and administers the fullness of the means of salvation. She is sent out by the Christ on a mission to the whole of the human race. Every particular Church is in fact catholic. It is formed by a community of Catholics who are in communion of faith and of the sacraments both with their Bishop, who is ordained in apostolic succession, and with the Church of Rome which presides in deep charity.

All human beings in various ways belong to or are ordered to the Catholic unity of the people of God. Fully incorporated into the Catholic Church are those who, possessing the Spirit of the Christ, are joined to the Church by the bonds of the profession of faith, the sacraments, ecclesiastical government and communion. There is a bond between all peoples which comes especially from the common origin and ultimate end of the entire human race. The Catholic Church recognizes that whatever is good or true in other Christian faiths and outside religions comes from God and is a reflection of his truth. As such the Church is ready and prepared for their acceptance of the Gospel and to act as a stimulus toward the unity of humanity in the Catholic Church of the Christ.

And Frank, having been confirmed in the Church to strengthen his baptismal grace, had now developed a deep sense of the spirit of the liturgy and he was ready and able to enter a special ministry in the

Church as assistant to the parish priest at the altar as an altar boy in the Mass. The effect of Frank's Confirmation was a special outpouring of the Holy Spirit like that of Pentecost. This outpouring impressed upon the young Frank's soul an indelible character which produced a greater growth in the grace of Baptism. It rooted Frank more deeply in divine sonship, binding him more firmly to the Christ and to the Church and reinvigorated the gifts of the Holy Spirit in his soul. It gave a special strength to witnessing the Catholic faith. Because Frank had already been baptized, he received the sacrament of Confirmation in the state of grace.

Frank had become a visible part of the congregation as a good server serving the Sunday Mass. He was also made ready to avail himself for other services his priest required of him. Frank as an altar boy meant serving God, his priest and his people at Mass. As a server Frank became very involved because the congregation was watching him closely. The young Frank understood that it was his fortune that he been chosen by God to give his service during the celebration of the liturgy. The liturgy is a public act of worship which the Church offers directly to God. The service of Frank the altar boy was extremely important because he was one of the closest persons to the Altar and to the Priest representing the Christ during the celebration of the Holy Mass and the administration of the Sacraments.

With the help of his parents the young Frank was chosen to be altar boy because he was an active member of his parish community and he believed in the teachings of the Holy Catholic Church. He knew all the prayers of the Holy Sacrifice of the Mass in Latin from memory and how to properly genuflect. He knew how to make the sign of the Cross and how to receive Holy Communion in the approved manner. His service to the Mass was a serious responsibility and the community was very grateful for the sacrifices of his time and talents.

Altar boys in the Roman Catholic Church are regarded as belonging to the clergy, having to learn Latin prayers, songs and to behave in a good manner and follow all the rules that are set for them. The altar boy helps the priest in those things which he does at the altar during the Sacrifice of the Mass and other liturgical events. He also sets a good example to the whole congregation, since he is highly visible and able to help the people in church to be more reverent. Many vocations to the priesthood have come from young men like Frank who served the priest at the altar.

In this way Frank drew closer to the Christ, which in turn enabled him to open himself to other believers, to journey with them in the Christ, to set demanding goals and to find the strength to achieve them. The closer Frank was to the altar, the more he remembered to speak with the Christ in daily prayer, the more he was nourished by the word and the body of the Christ, and the better able was he to go out to others, bringing them the gift that Frank had received, giving in turn with enthusiasm the joy he also received.

 O God, you had graciously called Frank
to serve You at Your Altar.
Grant him the graces that he needed
to serve You faithfully and wholeheartedly.
Grant too that while serving You,
May he follow the example of St. Tarcisius,
who died protecting the Eucharist,
and walk the same path that led him to Heaven.
St. Tarcisius, pray for him and for all servers.

Canon 7 - Infallibility and the sacrament of the Eucharist

The Angel's Chorus:
BLOOD IS TO WINE AS BREAD IS TO HOST,
CENTRE OF A THEOLOGY CONCEIVED INFALLIBLE,
THE FATHER, THE SON, AND THE HOLY GHOST,
IN A FAITH WHOSE TIDE SHOULD BE A FLOOD.

The Church is apostolic in her origin because she has been built on the foundation of the Apostles. She is apostolic in her teaching which grew out from the Apostles. She is apostolic by reason of her structure in that she teaches, sanctifies, guides and persuades until the Christ returns. The word Apostle means one who is sent. The Christ, the One sent by the Father, called to himself twelve of his disciples and appointed them as his Apostles, making them the chosen witnesses of his Resurrection and the foundation of his Church. He gave them the command to continue his own mission because as the Father has sent him, so does he send them with the promise that he will remain with them until the end of the world. And they have been succeeded through Catholic history by the bishops by means of the sacrament of Holy Orders, the mission and power of the Apostles. It is thanks to this transmission that the Church remains in communion of faith and life with her origin, having through the centuries carried on her apostolate for the spread of the Kingdom of the Christ on earth.

The Pope, Bishop of Rome and the Successor of Saint Peter, is the perpetual, visible source and foundation of the unity of the Church. He is the vicar of the Christ, the head of the College of bishops and pastor of the universal Church over which he has by divine institution full, supreme, immediate, and universal power. The College of bishops in union with the Pope, and never without him, exercise supreme and full authority within the Church. And since they are authentic witnesses of the apostolic faith and are invested with the authority of the Christ, the bishops in union with the Pope have the duty of proclaiming the Gospel faithfully and authoritatively to all. By means of a supernatural sense of faith, the people of God unfailingly adhere to this faith under the guidance of the living Magisterium of the Church.

At the Church's core is the doctrine of infallibility, no error, which is exercised when the Roman Pontiff, in virtue of his office as the Supreme Pastor of the Church, in union with the bishops especially when joined together in an Ecumenical Council, proclaim by a definitive act a doctrine pertaining to faith or morals. Infallibility is also exercised when the Pope and bishops in their ordinary Magisterium are in agreement in proposing a doctrine as definitive. Every one of the faithful must adhere to such teaching with the obedience of faith, as the Christ wished. Bishops therefore sanctify the Church by dispensing the grace of the Christ by their ministry of the word and the sacraments, especially the Holy Eucharist, and also by their prayers, their example and their work. Every bishop bears collegially the care for all particular churches and for the entire Church along with all the other bishops who are united to the Pope. A bishop to whom a particular church has been entrusted governs that church with the authority of his own sacred power which is ordinary and immediate and exercised in the name of the Christ, the Good Shepherd, in communion with the entire Church and under the guidance of the Successor of Peter.

Priests, in the persons of the Christ the Head and in the name of the Church, celebrate the Catholic Mystery in the liturgy, of which the principle sacrament of the Eucharist, or Mass, chiefly celebrated on Sunday which is the foundation and kernel of the entire liturgical year and has its culmination in the annual celebration of Easter, the feast of feasts. Through the exercise of the priestly office of the Christ the liturgy manifests in signs and brings about the sanctification of humankind. The public worship which is due to God is offered by the Mystical Body of the Christ, that is, by its head and by its members. The liturgy as the sacred action is the summit toward which the activity of the Church is directed and it is likewise the fount from which all her power flows.

In the Eucharist, the sanctifying action of God in all who worship him reaches their highest point. It contains the whole spiritual good of the Church, the Christ himself, Frank's own communion with divine life and the unity of the People of God as expressed by the Eucharist. Through the Eucharistic celebration Frank was already united with the liturgy of Heaven so that he might have a foretaste of eternal life. The Church, faithful to the command of her Lord, intrinsically celebrates the Eucharist, especially on Sunday, the day of the Resurrection of the Christ.

When Frank received the wheat bread and wine at Communion the whole substance of bread is changed into the substance of the Body of the Christ and of the whole substance of wine into the substance of his Blood. This change, called transubstantiation, is brought about in the Eucharistic prayer through the efficacy of the word of the Christ and by the action of the Holy Spirit. The outward characteristics of bread and wine remain unaltered, and yet what Frank consumed are the changed substances, created by the priest's words on behalf of the Christ. And when the wheat bread is broken is does not divide the Christ. He is present whole and entire in the bread and wine. And upon consumption the presence of the Christ continues in the Eucharist as long as the Eucharistic bread and wine subsist.

To receive Holy Communion, one must be fully incorporated into the Catholic Church and be in the state of grace, that is, not conscious of being in mortal sin. Anyone who is conscious of having committed a grave sin must first receive the sacrament of reconciliation through confession before going to Communion. Also important for those receiving Holy Communion is the spirit of recollection and prayer, observance of the fast prescribed by the Church, and an appropriate disposition of the body, in gesture and dress, as a sign of respect for the Christ. Holy Communion naturally increases Frank's union with the Christ and with his Church. It preserves and renews the life of grace received at Baptism and Confirmation, helping Frank develop a love for his God and his neighbour. It strengthens Frank in charity, wipes away his venial sins and preserves Frank from mortal sin in the future.

The Eucharist is a pledge of future glory because it fills Frank with every grace and heavenly blessing. It fortifies Frank for his pilgrimage in his life and makes him yearn for eternal life. It unites Frank to the Christ seated at the right hand of the Father, to the Church in Heaven and to the Blessed Virgin and all the saints. In the Eucharist, the breaking of the bread provides the medicine of immortality, the antidote for death and is the food which makes Frank live forever in the Christ.

Canon 8 - And Frank pleased his family by thinking aloud about becoming a priest

The Angel's Chorus:
SEEDS ARE SOWN FOR FRANK TO BE A PRIEST,
SLOW AT FIRST AND THEN HIS CALLING IS A FIRE,
HE'LL BE THE CENTRE OF EVERY SUNDAY FEAST,
SERVING GOD'S CHILDREN IN THEIR NEEDS.

It was the teenage Frank who openly articulated that the sacrament of Holy Orders was made for him. He will be set apart as one from the many for the purpose of serving God through the priesthood. Through a special gift of the Holy Spirit, this sacrament enables him when ordained as God's chosen servant, to exercise a sacred power in his name with the authority of the Christ for the service of the People of God. To the delight of his parents Frank spoke of this in halting fragments over Sunday lunches.

The anointing of the Spirit seals Frank as priest with an indelible, spiritual character that configures him to the Christ and enables him to act in the name of the Christ the Head. As a co-worker of the order of Bishops he is consecrated to preach the Gospel, to celebrate divine worship, especially the Eucharist from which his ministry draws its strength, and to be a shepherd of the faithful.

This sacrament can only be validly received by the baptized Frank. The Church recognizes herself as bound by the choices made by the Christ Himself; because he established his Church with men only. Intimacy between the Virgin Mary and she, the Church can only be through men. Yet no man can demand to receive the sacrament of Holy Orders, but must be judged suitable for the ministry by the authorities of the Church. It is always necessary to be celibate for the episcopacy and the men who are chosen fully intend, in the name of the Christ, to continue to live a celibate life for the kingdom of Heaven. The sacrament yields a special outpouring of the Holy Spirit which configures the recipient to the Christ in his triple office as Priest, Prophet, and King, according to the respective degrees of the sacrament. When a celibate man is ordained to the priesthood, he is conferred an indelible spiritual character which cannot be repeated and is eternal.

The priesthood and sacrifice are reciprocal terms, proving the Divine origin of the Catholic priesthood, thus showing that the Eucharistic Sacrifice of the Mass came with the beginnings and essence of Catholicism. Rightly, there is an intimate connection between the Sacrifice of the Mass and the priesthood. Sacrifice and priesthood by Divine ordinance are so inseparable that they are found together under all laws.

The Sacrifice of the Mass indicates only one side of the priesthood; the other side is revealed in the power of forgiving sin, the exercise of which for the priesthood is a necessary for the power of consecration and renewal. Like the general power to bind and to loose, the power of remitting and containing sins was solemnly bestowed on the Church by the Christ.

Accordingly, the Catholic priesthood has the indisputable right to trace its origin in this respect to the Divine Founder of the Church. If anyone shall say that in the New Testament there is no visible and external priesthood or any power of consecrating and offering the Body and Blood of the Christ, as well as of remitting and containing sins, but merely the office and bare ministry of preaching the Gospel, let them be mercilessly scorned. The priesthood forms so indispensable a foundation of Catholicism that its removal would entail the destruction of the whole edifice. Catholicism without the priesthood cannot be the true Church of the Christ.

It is clear that the Catholic clergy alone are entitled to the designation 'priest', since they alone have a true and real sacrifice to offer, the Holy Mass. The powers of the Catholic priest are intimately connected with the sacramental character, indelibly imprinted on his soul. Together with this character is conferred, not only the power of offering up the Sacrifice of the Mass and the power of forgiving sins, but also the authority to administer extreme unction and, as the regular minister, solemn baptism. To the priestly office also belongs the faculty of administering the ecclesiastical blessings.

Through the Catholic priesthood, there has spread to all nations and brought into full bloom over time and lands, with the force of righteous persuasion morality, wealth, science, art, and industry. If religion in general is the mother of all culture, Catholicism must be acknowledged as the source, measure, and nursery of all true civilization. The Church, the oldest and most successful teacher of mankind, has in each century done pioneer service in all departments of culture. Through her organs, the priests and other members of religious orders, the Church has carried the light of Faith to all lands, banished the darkness of paganism, and with the Gospel brought the blessings of Catholic morality and education.

In the wake of the Catholic Church there follows her inseparable companion, preaching; the combination of these two forms being the indispensable preliminary condition for the continuation and vitality of all higher civilizations. The decadence of culture has always been heralded by a reign of unbelief and immorality. Frank will learn that what the Church has accomplished in the course of the centuries for the raising of the standard of morality, in the widest sense, is by the inculcation of the Ten Commandments, that pillar of human society, by promulgating the commandment of love of God and one's neighbour, by preaching purity in single, married, and family life, by waging war upon superstition and evil customs, by the practice of the three counsels of

35

voluntary poverty, obedience, and in itself perfect purity. The Church has held out for all to see that the 'imitation of the Christ' is the ideal of Catholic perfection. Frank will learn that the Church's record of twenty centuries of its accomplishments are simply wonderful. And in the next twenty centuries its achievements will be even greater.

Intimately related with the morally good is the idea of the true and the beautiful, the object of all science and art. And at all times the Catholic clergy have shown themselves patrons of science and the arts, partly by their own achievements in these fields and partly by their encouragement and support of the work of others. And Frank, lover of poetry, will feel even more at one with the Church. That theology as a science should find its warmest home among the clergy was to be expected. And had it not been for the monks and clerics, the poetics of ancient classical literature would have been surely lost.

Canon 9 - Frank contemplating the priesthood as sinner

The Angel's Chorus:
TO KNOW EVIL IS TO KNOW ALL ABOUT SIN,
A HUMBLE PRIEST GIVES PENANCE BEST,
GOD'S LOVE IS FOR GOOD CATHOLICS TO WIN,
STILL THE DEVIL HAS MUCH TEMPTING TO DO.

Frank began to confess his sins at the suitable age of seven in light of Pope Pius the Tenth's edict. And since the age of seven he became increasingly comfortable with the sacrament of confession and penance. By his teens Frank became well aware of how much of a sinner he is given the number of confessions he has made and the amount of penance he has received. And his guilt will have no end unless he repents. He is comforted to know that he is no different to other teenagers of the Catholic faith and their parents, in that they are also frequent penitents. Penance in an important pathway for many young Catholic males contemplating the priesthood, as it lays the groundwork for a deep understanding of the power of forgiveness when they as priests perform their role as frequent forgivers on God's behalf.

When Frank sins it is a voluntary act inspired by the Devil, the originator of sin. The Devil, as an operator in Frank's unconscious just as God is, is ever present to disrupt his human vulnerability as a young man with feelings and passions. The only successful defence against this is penance, prayer and faith in God.

The young Frank regularly confessed his pride in himself, his covetousness of his sibling's toys, his teenage lust, his hatred of his older sister's teasing, his anger towards his parents, his gluttony at the dinner table, his envy of his classmates and his sloth at study. Because of these and more, Frank was well on the way to understanding the power of forgiveness.

Frank, whose thoughts turned more and more toward the priesthood, must consider the root causes of his sins. His mentors have told him that the causes are actually interior and exterior. The principal interior causes of his sin are his ignorance, his passions and his malice. His ignorance comes from his defective reasoning, while his passions are on the part of his sensual appetites for life, and his malice on the part of his will. His sins are from certain malice when the will sins of its own accord and not under the influence of ignorance or passion.

The exterior causes of Frank's sins are the Devil and humanity, who move Frank to sin by means of suggestion, temptation and bad example. God is not the cause of his sin. God directs all things to Himself and is the end of all His actions, and he cannot be the cause of evil otherwise his existence would be a causal contradiction. Of whatever entity there is in sin as an action, Frank is part or the whole of sin's consequences. Frank's sinful will is the cause of his teenage disorder. One sin of his may be the cause of another connecting one to another and then another. Frank's regular ignorance, jealousy, and concupiscence are the consequences of original sin.

The first effect of Frank's sinning is to avert him from his true last end, depriving his soul of sanctifying grace. Frank's sinful state is voluntary and imputable to him, and the guilt remains until satisfaction is made through penance. Frank's state of sin is habitual and is demonstrated by his wavering aversion to God. This state of aversion carries with it the deprivation of grace and charity, without which Frank will not achieve a happy supernatural end. The stains of Frank's sins are solely from his deprivation of sanctifying grace caused by his sinning. Frank, when he sins, deprives his soul of the beauty of God's grace. And in Frank's unconscious how the devil laughs!

When Frank sins he finds out their penalties through his contrition made at confession. His sins are the cause of this obligation. Frank must fear that should his earthly contrition not satisfy the justice of God as preached by his beloved Catholic Church then eternal suffering awaits. The punishments of Frank's future life are proportioned to the sin committed, and it is Frank's obligation to undergo punishments for his sins. If Frank's sins are mortal and remain unrepented for, his future life will be divided into the pain of loss, the deprivation of the beatific vision of God, and the pain of sense while suffering in Hell.

Frank's teenage sins are probably venial, though they are awful to him. Sins are called venial because they are pardonable and the punishment is temporal. They are distinguished from mortal sin on the part of the disorder. By mortal sin humans are entirely averted from God, their true last end, by instead seeing their last end as something created in their imagination, that is, no heaven, no soul, no after life consciousness. The true nature of mortal sin is contrary to the eternal law, and is repugnant to the primary end of the law, immortality.

It is the Devil, created by God, who is the cause of sin, either directly or indirectly. Sin is a violation of order, and because only God can directly order good things unto himself, since this is his ultimate end, he cannot be the direct cause of Frank's sins. If God withdrew grace from Frank to prevent him sinning it would make Frank the sole cause of his sins and the quality of his remorse would be entirely his own. It is God's will that his grace be anathema to the Devil. Outwardly God would appear to be under no obligation to impede Frank's sinning. But inwardly he inclines Frank to sin because his divine judgment allows it, for then he can exercise his justice in punishment of Frank's sins through penance as expressed in confession. As God only directly causes exterior works that are good in themselves, it is the combined evil wills of humanity and the Devil which abuses that goodness, for, by giving humanity free will has he given them the power to accomplish what is evil.

God would not have permitted evil had he not been almighty enough to bring good out of evil. God's end in creating this universe is himself, and good and evil serve his ends, and there shall be finally a restoration of violated order through Divine justice. None of Frank's sins will be without its punishment. God has provided a remedy for Frank's sinning through his love and goodness despite Frank's lapses in ingratitude towards the Incarnation of His Divine Son. And God has provided, by instituting Frank's Church to interpret for them his law, through the sacraments and the various channels of grace, a complete remedy for sin as a means to unite with God in Heaven upon death, the ultimate of his law.

For Frank to become closer to God he must try to better understand his sins through his acts of contrition. Sin impresses within him a watchful fear, a fear of his own powers, a fear, if left to his own devices, of an ultimate and permanent fall from grace. By necessity Frank must seek God's help and grace that he may stand firm when faced with his contradictory feelings of fear and love of God, in order to make progress in his spiritual life. The Catholic priest's teaching is the only one which places sin in its true light, justifying the Church's condemnation of sin in imitation of the Christ.

The Catholic Church continues to strive to impress upon her children the sense of the awfulness of sin so that they may fear it and avoid it. Frank is a fallen human, and his spiritual life on earth is in warfare. Sin is Frank's enemy. He cannot avoid sin using his own strength, but with God's grace he can. If he can place no obstacle to the workings of grace Frank can avoid all deliberate sin. But he will need the Catholic Church's help. If he has the misfortune to sin, but seeks God's grace and is pardoned in confession with a contrite and humble heart, God will not repel him.

Sins remedied by grace, which is given to Frank by God in the Catholic Church, through the teachings of his only-begotten Son, will help Frank restore his love for God making him once again a child of God and heir to a place in Heaven. Where the Catholic doctrine of the creation of humanity is recognised as superior in everything, where its dogmas of redemption and grace in reparation of Frank's sins are kept in mind, there is no discouragement for him. Left to himself Frank will fall, but by his daily closeness to God and the seeking of his help, Frank will learn to understand his struggles against his sinning, and if he remains true to his battles he shall be crowned in Heaven.

Frank has learnt much from what he has been taught; that the works of the flesh, manifest in adultery, fornication, uncleanness, lasciviousness, idolatry, witchcraft, hatred, wrath, strife, seditions, heresies, drunkenness, and such like, if committed by him and in any combination of these, and where there is no contrition, he shall not inherit the kingdom of God. Frank's Church also teaches him that the sins of anger, blasphemy, envy, hatred, malice, murder, neglect of Sunday obligation, sins against faith, against the vulnerable, incredulity against God or heresy, atheism, sins against hope, obstinate despair against salvation, the idea that one can wholly live without God, sins against love, sins against the body, indifference towards charity, ingratitude, hatred of God, all constitute mortal gravity. They are based on the Christ's interpretation of the gravity of the Ten Commandments. Grave sins are the ones which cry most to Heaven for God's vengeance.

Canon 10 - Frank as eager Celibate

The Angel's Chorus:
SEX IS EVERYTHING FOR FRANK TO FEAR,
IT IS TOO DIABOLICAL FOR A PERFECT PRIEST,
HIS VIRGINITY HE WILL BE HOLDING DEAR,
THE DEVIL FANCIES FONDLING IT WITH A HEX.

Celibacy is the renunciation of marriage which in turn suppresses sexual desire to then create the most perfect celebration of chastity. The teenage Frank was obviously too young to marry, and since the Christ was perfectly chaste Frank, as a future Catholic priest, would also be celibate, since he would be already in this state. And yet he is to anxiously question again and again this burden while serving God. It will only when he fully understands the vow of chastity will he be able to bind himself forever with God in the ministry of the priesthood. Upon his ordination Frank will be bound unequivocally with God. He cannot marry. If he breaks the vow of chastity it will not only be a grievous sin, but Frank would also incur the additional guilt of a terrible sacrilege.

The celibate Frank is to seek the graces belonging to the Christ, so that he may yet please God. If Frank had a wife, he would seek nothing except that of the real world and what pleases his wife and his loving energy would divide him between earthly things and God. The Church, from its earliest consciousness, has always seen itself as the Virgin Bride of the Christ, the prime worshiper of the Virgin Mother of God, and it was plainly fitting that this virgin Church should be served by a virgin priesthood. The priest is an impartation of the Holy Spirit in the divinely-instituted Sacrament of Orders. Virginity is the special privilege of the priesthood. The conviction that virginity possesses a higher sanctity and a clearer spiritual intuition is an instinct planted deep by God in the heart of every Catholic priest. Clean must Frank be when he is handling the vessels of the Christ.

42

Frank as priest will be someone who sacrifices himself for the sake of his parishioners. He will have no children of his own but instead all in his parish will be his children. His flock will also know that his small wants will be catered for by his Church, so that he can devote all his time and influence to them his sheep. And when he is finished with his daily duties Frank will return to quiet study, and nothing of the distracting world will disturb his prayerful thoughts.

There will be certain times in his life in which Frank will hear himself both be called and condemned by the Christ's absolute perfection, and this will only inspire him to real humility, with that strong sense of his own deep wretchedness causing in him an ardent yearning for the Christ's return. He must always aim for that pure love which renounces life. For Frank to obey the Christ and do his bidding he must be ever watchful of this world with all its desires and passions. He must not lapse into discouragement and despair. With the help of the Holy Spirit and in vigilant perseverance sustained by prayer and self-discipline, Frank as priest will indeed win victory over himself. He shall seek his strength in the Christ and accept that he must break with the surrounding world in order to truly serve Him. While waiting for the Christ to return and make the world holy, Frank will live in this world accepting the many sacrifices in his dedicated priestly life so that his suffered waiting will have meaning.

Celibacy is the chief sign that will remind Frank of the Christ's absolute demands upon him, of the Christ's liberating return, of the economy of the kingdom of Heaven, Frank's breaking with the world, with the flesh and the normal order of Creation, and, with joy in his heart, to renounce his bodily passions for a pure love of the Christ. Celibacy dictates that a perfect relationship with the Christ entails sacrificial demands, so that Frank's life is one of a complete and lifelong sexual faithfulness seeding a pure heart and mind. Celibacy is the ultimate way for Frank to obey the

Christ's invitation to come after him, to deny himself and take up his cross and follow him. When Frank finally loses his life for the Christ's sake, he will find it in him. He will need to be in the world without being of the world, to deal with the problems of world and live as though he has no dealings with it, for this form of world will be soon passing away. The celibate Frank will be free to proclaim the gospel and to act as sign of the kingdom of God to come.

As a celibate priest Frank, in performing his difficult missions, will be so much freer than a married man who has family responsibilities. He can leave for anywhere, at any moment, in response to the Church's urgent requests, which the married man cannot easily do. Because Frank cannot marry, he will be free from normal family troubles, and it will also be an advantage to live in celibacy should martyrdom reach him. A martyred life devoted to the priesthood and to the many anxieties over obedience to the Christ and to the mission which Frank has been called to partake in, is a life created to exist within the two orders of necessity, that of the sexual joy of marriage and that of the spiritual joy of the Church, both of which having been willed by God.

Frank's celibate life, although depriving him of conjugal intimacy and fatherhood in the physical order, will allow him to completely offer himself to his flock, for their salvation and to their sanctification. Having no exclusive love, the celibate Frank will be at the disposal of all, and he will have the time and inner freedom to serve his parishioners in charity. He will give much time to those who wish to confide in him and he can look after all who need his sustained support. And being alone he will inspire trust from all who wish to confide in him, the vulnerable, and in particular children. When guided by the Holy Spirit in directing souls, Frank need not have experienced every human situation himself, because as celibate he will be a spiritual father to those who willingly confide in him.

44

Frank's celibacy will be in honour of the Christ's earthly virginal flesh, establishing an intimate relationship with him. The celibate Frank will be consecrated directly with the Christ in his complete humanity, soul and body. And once he has given himself completely to the Christ, honouring his flesh, united with him in every aspect of his human nature, Frank will not be able to breach this union without an act of infidelity. By consecrating his body and soul to the Christ Frank is pleasing him with all of his life and being. Every aspect of his priestly life will be in accord with this effort. And not only will he seek to live in purity of heart and body, but his behaviour, his words, his relationships, shall reveal fully the beauty of Frank's priestly vocation.

Frank will also be seeking to please the Christ in prayer and contemplation. His own celibacy not only signifies what he is as priest, but it will demand that he be in a state of continual dependence on God. In his loneliness, the Christ's love will fill his need for love, and in prayer he will find every joy. And the Virgin Mary will be his divine example in that she had consecrated her body and spirit to God alone, in an act of perfect dependence. Frank will learn to love deeply the Virgin Mary because his virginity depends entirely upon his intimate relationship with her.

The life of prayer and contemplation expressing this dependence on the Christ and the Virgin will assume a major role in Frank's future priestly life. The lonely celibate priest naturally puts all his trust in God, to live in unique dependence on and friendship with him and, because of this, he will devote much of his time in prayer. In the Church, the beauty of the liturgy is directly related to the priest's desire to praise the Christ. Liturgical worship expresses love and gratitude for him and his sacrifice. Regular liturgical and contemplative life in the Church, and the Divine Office which Frank will be bound to recite will bring him ever closer to the Christ in contemplation. The Christ had no other bride than the Church, and the Christ's disciple the priest has no better earthly companion than his bride, the Church. By being close to the Christ and listening to him the Christ's voice will fill him with joy in prayer and in contemplation, and there it will be, Frank's perfect happiness.

Whenever Frank feels utter loneliness, he will remind himself that there is a promise which will correspond to his commitment. In the Church he will find a community of all the saints, today and forever. He will draw strength and courage from those who, like him, have willed to follow the Christ in this special vocation of the celibate life. He need not think of himself as being alone in the Church and in the fellowship of the saints since he is the Christ's friend. He is a member of the body of the Christ, and all the members of this body are bound together in absolute indissoluble unity. In this state of nobility Frank will live an honourable and beautiful life, with a loving simplicity to nourish it all the way to his death.

As celibate Frank will also be detached from a troubled world waiting for a striking sign of a new order, for this one is slowly passing away. A consecrated celibacy is a sign of the Resurrection and of the kingdom of God which is drawing near, for in the Resurrection and the kingdom there will be neither marrying nor giving in marriage. Celibacy, in the Church, thus draws attention to the new order of the gospel, whereas marriage has its roots in the old order. In the kingdom of God, the fullness of love will be such that no one will feel the need for sexual intimacy any more. On the contrary, it would seem like a diminution of love. Thus, Frank as priest will be the sign of the fullness of love which will come when the Christ's kingdom comes again.

Celibacy also relates to the resurrection of the dead because it is a sign of eternity, of incorruptibility, of a pure life. Marriage has as its natural end the procreation of children, assuring the continuance of the human race and the creation of new beings, since human beings are fated to die because of sin. Frank's celibate state will promise life in eternity and a life with the angels, a life as a perfect follower of the Christ. The ministry of the gospel in contemplative prayer at the feet of the Christ, in proclaiming the coming kingdom of God, and in offering the sacrifice of the Eucharist, is a perfect description of Frank's future priesthood. As a celibate Frank will be called to offer his whole mind, spirit, and body in response to the Christ, who offered his whole being in every act while on earth culminating in his total gift on the Cross. He'll be an imitator of the Christ, and live in love with the Christ, as the Christ loves him.

It will be important for Frank as priest to cultivate healthy friendships with women. In this way he will further understand God through the different approaches, concerns, and feelings found in women. It will be essential that Frank as priest take the necessary time to get to know women on a deeper level, though they are not perfect like the Virgin Mary. But these friendships will require proper boundaries. Luckily for Frank as a consecrated celibate, God as the Christ is his deepest and most intimate friend. And the Virgin Mary is always there to meet his sensual needs. Deep and well-formed friendships with women will help round off Frank's deep and well-formed friendship with the Christ. Frank's love for the Christ will be seen in how he conducts his friendships with women. Nothing will be withheld about his self when he totally entrusts himself to women. There will be many friendships in which Frank as priest has willingly accepted everything offered to him by his flock. Love, for Frank, will be expressed in his desire to suffer the sufferings of others and to share in their joys. His joy will enter unto them so that their joy is complete.

Loving those whom the Christ loves, will not only allow the celibate Frank to experience the Christ's profound love for others, but also will allow him to experience the Christ's love for himself. Frank's celibacy will offer him the opportunity to provide a self-giving love to many people and in doing so expand the ability to receive the love of God through them. He will experience a deep sense of intimacy with God in offering the sacraments while discerning the power and love of the Christ working within himself through these gracious gifts from Heaven. And through these same Sacraments, he will also feel a deep intimacy with the Bride of the Christ, the Church that he is serving and laying his life down for.

The celibate Frank will live, by God's personal invitation, in a relationship with him on Earth which is exactly the same as the one which will be experienced in the kingdom of Heaven. Frank's true call to celibacy is discerned through the discovery of one thing, a burning desire to love the Christ that will not be suppressed by anything outside this intimate union with him. This is a love which will make Frank forget all the other loves in the world. For when the call to celibacy for the kingdom of Heaven finds an echo in Frank's human soul, in the conditions of his temporal life, it will not difficult for him to sense that there a particular sensitiveness within his human spirit which will allow him to share the future resurrection of humanity, born again, and abode in the loving arms of God.

Canon 11 - The Calling to the Priesthood

The Angel's Chorus:
OBTUSE IS THE PRIESTHOOD BEFORE IT IS FIRM,
THE THINGS PRIESTS DO NOBODY ELSE CAN,
THEIR FAITH ALWAYS MAKES THE EVIL SQUIRM,
EXCEPT WHEN THERE IS SEXUAL ABUSE.

God's call for Frank to enter the priesthood had now occupied his thinking for a long time and the words he heard in his head were no longer from the urgings of his parents and his parish priest. It was this nagging feeling that he should become a priest, and which seemed to come from nowhere, uninvited; an idea he couldn't get out of his mind. Frank's desire grew in his teenage years and no pretty girl who liked him could shake the feeling out of him. And not only his parents but also his extended family, except his older sister, could see it in him as well. He felt unease at first, but then he saw the vocation as something natural to him. He enjoyed participating in the sacraments as an altar boy, and eventually an inner peace grew in him when thinking about the priesthood. And although he tried academically and on the sporting field, he knew they were not for him. He imagined himself as a priest and it seemed to fit, imagining loving to do what a priest does, to celebrate Mass, to preach, to baptise and to visit the sick. And when once he did kiss a girl, he did not enjoy the experience. He felt he would lose control of himself. It is more freeing if he were to lose control for God.

He had this feeling that he couldn't hold back his love for God. It was not enough for him to just work and plod along and say a few prayers and be nice to people. He felt that he wanted to give his whole heart, though he was not sure as to how or why, even though he doubted whether he was capable of being a priest, or that he was worthy. The priesthood might be too much of an ideal for him, and he doubted whether he was morally good enough.

When Frank spoke of these feelings to his parish priest, he assured Frank in confidence that how Frank felt was normal for a teenager with true humility, and though Frank had a healthy sense of his limitations, he had a high sense of the dignity of the priesthood. Frank's feelings of unworthiness was a sign that he had a true appreciation for the priesthood, and that he will be open to asking for God's help and the help of the Church.

He thought of what else he might do in life but he felt he was not equipped to do them. His priest told him that even though he is with sin, through his acts of contrition there is returned to him the rich grace endowed to him by God. The idea for the priesthood also came to Frank as the result of deliberation according to the principles of his Catholic reasoning and his deep faith. At one time Frank thought he felt a supernatural light pierce into his soul.

Deep down, in the normal course of Frank's young life, there was an ever-deepening personal relationship with the Christ, who in return gives his love and care for Frank. God answered his prayers by saying in Frank's unconscious that the priesthood is what he had created Frank for. How Frank might best respond to the gift of the priesthood his whole life would require him to take his faith even most seriously. Frank found that he wanted to pray more. Frank also became more honest about his faults and failings, and he held a strong desire to go to confession more often than in the past. He was earnestly learning more about his Catholic faith, and his love for the Christ and the Church was ever growing.

In Frank's prayers, his daydreaming, his imagination, in his reading of the gospels, he had found himself, with no conscious effort, coming closer to the idea of the priesthood. At mass certain scripture passages spoken by the parish priest Frank was sure were directed at him, passage about the works of the Christ, the mission of the Gospels, the sacrifices made. His parish priest demonstrated a goodness and holiness in his demeanour which attracted Frank to him. His life seems a life worth living, in a special way that spoke to Frank.

Frank had made himself a list, on the advice from his priest, which he could question and correct at any time.

To be or not be called.

By his commitment to his Catholic faith: a love for the Christ, for the Sacraments, for the People of God.
By his love and respect for the Catholic Church and for her teachings, and a desire to share that faith with others, even when he found some things more difficult to believe than others.
By his commitment to the commandments, and to living a moral life, even if he is weak and struggles with his desires.
By his maturity so that he might live outside of normal society in the seminary and later a parish residence, and to engage in pastoral work, getting on comfortably with different people.
That he is in prayerful dialogue with God and with the Church in the discernment of his vocation.
That he loves the Eucharist.
That he longs to administer the sacraments to the people of God.
That he hungers to build up the Church and promote bonds of profound ecclesial communion especially in the dynamics of parish life.
That he is driven to be a servant-leader and spiritual father to his brothers and sisters in the faith.
That he has a real zest to live to the priesthood's ultimate consequence of a deep-rooted experience of a discipleship in the Christ.
That his friendship with the Christ is intimate who has taken the Church as his bride, and serve her exclusively and unconditionally throughout the rest of his life.

That his heart is irrevocably set and fixated on the Christ from whom he has perceived an undeniable invitation and calling, and to follow him more intimately as his servant.

That his capacity to give and receive love is ever deepening.

That he is developing self-discipline in the face of worldly temptation.

That he is gaining a degree of self-mastery over his feelings and emotions which will enable him to be appropriately vulnerable, to manifest empathy, to communicate emotion with prudence and balance, and to share and receive appropriate gestures of affirmation and affection.

That he commits himself, amidst the usual temptations and struggles, to strive in earnest for life-long abstinence from any deliberate sexual gratification.

That he lives a sustained life of personal prayer allowing himself to be drawn into a deeper desire for a transformative union with the Trinity and with that a deeper, affectively mature, and fruitful communion with the Church.

That he is willing and able to grow in his prayer life.

That he is committed to grow and meet whatever God may bring his way.

That he can face the cross and find in it a way to his personal resurrection.

That in all this, he trusts God to guide him.

That outside the Church there is no salvation.

Yet in Frank's deeper conscience there lingers a discomfort around his spiritual relationship with his parish priest. Since Frank has been an altar boy there had been occasions, in the privacy of the rectory and under the seal of the confessional, when his Holy Father instructed Frank to show him his genitals. He wished to inspect them for their purity. Then upon arousal his Holy Father would stroke Frank until ejaculation, and after his Holy Father had cleaned Frank up, he pleaded with him to assist with his. The Holy Father told Frank that God had allowed them this intimate and special friendship: a spiritual bond had formed and it was unbreakable. And it was not for others to judge whether their intimacy was sinful. It was God's judgement alone that mattered. Frank felt he could never tell anyone, except God in prayer. And so far, Frank has been unable to reconcile his dignity with that of his Holy Father's, and to understand the grace which God's love has brought to them both.

Canon 12 - Doing Good while being perfect when doing Good

The Angel's Chorus:
LIFE IS BEST LIVED IN THE CATHOLIC WAY,
ITS INSTRUCTION IS READY FOR THE NEEDY,
THE PRIEST IS GIVEN THE GOD-SPOKEN SAY,
OVER IGNORANCE THE CHURCH SAYS IS RIFE.

By doing good Frank permanently binds himself to a Catholic path which will lead him to perfection. He will be bound by the vow to refrain from worldly affairs, though lawful and considered, in order that he more freely give himself to God. Frank will never be a hypocrite and sin, not because he is not perfect, but because he is ever ready to sincerely take the Godly path to perfection. His religious life, based on the great precept of the love of God and one's neighbour, will maintain for Frank a loftiness in not only his canonical or juridical aspect, but also it will be of great spiritual meaning.

To maintain this Frank will need to avoid the concupiscence of the eyes or the desire of exterior things, the concupiscence of the flesh, and a pride of life, and the love of independence. These he will renounce and then he will offer to God exterior goods through poverty, his body and his heart through religious chastity, and his will through obedience. There is nothing more that he need offer and, if he does not take back what he has given, but practices ever more perfectly, with a greater love of God and of his neighbour, he will truly offer to God a perfect sacrifice. His Catholic life has already been an act of worship, renewing his promises with greater merit than when he made them for the first time. Such a merit is expected to grow in him along with his charity and the other virtues, and his consecration to God will then become increasingly intimate and complete, a prelude to eternal life.

Frank as priest will reach this goal through the imitation of the Christ, who is the way, the truth, and the life. By the grace of personal union with the Word, the Christ's nature was wholly consecrated, his intellect rendered infallible, his will impeccable; in him all thoughts, every act of the will, and all the emotions of his sensibility were from God and were directed to God. The sovereign dominion of God has never been as completely exercised as in the sacred humanity of the Christ as Savoir.

It is, that Frank will answer God's call to follow Him, but, whereas the Christ came from above, Frank is coming from below, from the region of sin, from his sinful mother's womb, from disturbances repressed. He will need to progressively separate himself from all that is inferior in order to consecrate himself more and more intimately to God. He is to seek the things that are above, where the Christ is sitting at the right hand of God, and mind the things that are above, and not the things that are upon the earth. Frank's priestly life will be with the Christ in God. As priest Frank cannot taste the things of the world, for he is dead to the sinful world around him.

Frank as priest will be consecrated to celebrate the Holy of the Holy and in doing so, he will faithfully and devoutly offer himself up in sacrifice to God, so that he can show himself to be blameless. His burden will be heavy, but he will be bound by a stricter bond of discipline and obliged to seek greater perfection of sanctity. He ought to be adorned with all virtues and set the example of a good life to others. His conversation won't be with the popular and in the common ways of ordinary people, but with the angels in Heaven, and with other perfect priests gracing the earth.

The priesthood promises Frank that when he celebrates the holy sacrifice of the Mass he will be like the figure of the Christ who offered Himself as saviour of the world. Frank as priest will be conscious of the greatness of his functions, and he ought to strive for an ever-closer union in heart and soul with the Christ, the most sacred of victims. For Frank to mount the altar steps without the firm will to grow in charity would be a gross hypocrisy. His Communion should be substantially more fervent each day by reason of a greater promptness of the will in the service of God, since the sacrament of the Eucharist ought not only to preserve but to increase charity in humanity. By serving the Christ in the sacrament of the altar Frank will be required to develop a greater inward holiness than that which is ordinarily required.

Frank will say the Divine Prayers with dignity, attention, and true piety. These great prayers of the Church are the accompaniment of the Sacrifice of the Mass. They precede it as a prelude. Frank's priesthood will be as the spouse of the Christ from dawn until dark, and it will be a great honour to be so. During prayerful recitation the great intentions of the Church for the pacification of the world through its extension of the kingdom of the Christ, will always remain in Frank's mind.

Frank will have the special obligation to tend to perfection that he may accomplish his functions well in relation to the mystical body of the Christ. Nothing will lead the faithful more surely to true piety than the good example of Frank as priest. The eyes of people will rest on him as on a mirror of perfection. Thus, Frank will order his life, his manners, his exterior, his gestures, and his words in such a way that he always preserves the gravity, moderation, and piety of one who is the imitator of the Christ. Frank will be expected to be free from attachment to worldly things, instead willingly bestowing them upon the poor. He ought obey his Bishop and be the servant of the faithful in spite of difficulties and calamities.

The need for this perfection will show especially in Frank's work of preaching. His preaching will be living and fruitful, and he must speak from the abundance of his heart and proceed from the fullness of contemplation, from the living, penetrating, delightful faith in the mystery of the Christ, in the infinite value of the Mass, in the value of sanctifying grace and of eternal life. Frank must preach like a saviour of souls, and he should work incessantly for the salvation of many, many souls. Because of this Frank's priesthood will not be in vain, nor will he fail the spiritual expectations of the Christ and his Church.

As for confession and spiritual direction, Frank must have a burning and luminous soul, a hunger and thirst for the justice of God; otherwise his ministry will be a danger to him. If life does not ascend, it descends, and so that his ministry won't descend, his life must ever rise like a flame. Even as the Church sees to Frank's basic needs, he must demonstrate to his parish how poor he is in his dwelling, in his clothing, and in his food, for he is their humble servant only. He will also need to be humble of spirit and of heart in his relations with God. The greater his poverty the more he will glorify God and the more spiritually will he guide his flock. Frank must be able to immolate himself through silence, prayer, work, penance, suffering, and death. The more Frank as priest dies for others, the more life he will obtain for him to then give it to others. He will be like good bread; he is a man who is consumed. And most gladly will Frank expend himself for others' souls, and by loving them more he will be loved less.

The true calling for Frank as priest therefore is to live as though a crucified man.

It will be necessary that Frank, who is to teach and instruct the people in virtue, be holy in all things, and be in no way reprehensible. When Frank is to convince another of sin, he himself must be temporarily free from sin. When he seeks to admonish others to live well, he must correct himself, so that in all things he himself may furnish an example of living and incite all to do good work by teaching and work. And learned in doctrine and speech, he will also instruct others and teach his flock, and repulse adversaries who, unless they can be refuted and convicted, will easily pervert the hearts of the simple. His speech will be pure, simple, open, full of gravity and honesty, sweetness and grace, entreating of the mystery of the law, of the doctrine of faith, of the virtue of love, of the discipline of justice.

Frank will also have charity which is super-eminent among all gifts, without which all virtue is nothing. Charity is, indeed, the guardian of chastity. Humility, moreover, is the place where it is kept. He will likewise have, among all these things, eminent chastity. Thus, as his mind is given to the Christ, he should be spotless and be free from carnal impurity. Among these things, it behoves him to take care of the poor with careful distribution, to feed the hungry, receive pilgrims, redeem sinners, advocate for the dispossessed, show prudent care in all things, provide with careful discretion. Hospitality should likewise be outstanding in him, that he may receive all with benignity and charity.

Canon 13 - Getting to know God

The Angel's Chorus:
TO BEST KNOW GOD IS IN CONTINUOUS PRAYER,
OUTDOORS AND INDOORS IN EVERY WHICH WAY,
UNBELIEVERS THINK PRAYING IS A BLANK STARE,
WHEN FRANK FAILS, HE'LL KNOW WHAT TO DO.

As priest Frank is called to be committed to learning all he can about his God and sharing his intimate knowledge with others, particularly through the sacraments. In his relationship with God Frank will love and be loved by God, in an intimate and transcendent way, and this relationship will be an ongoing and life-giving process, and always beginning with prayer, Frank's anchor. His personal prayer is a time of solace and silence in God's presence. It is also a time of words; words spoken in the manner that best nurtures Frank's personal relationship with God. It is crucial that Frank spend as much time as possible in personal prayer. In the person of the Christ Frank, in presiding over the Eucharist, shall give homilies steeped in wisdom and inspiration in a manner that is the Christ like. These moments in the Eucharist are the most important in the life of the Mass.

In knowing God through the eyes of his faith Frank will be better placed to embrace the troubled human condition. His role will involve the joyful celebration of new life at baptisms and weddings, and sharing the grief of those who mourn the loss of loved ones. Priesthood will call upon Frank to sit with the infirm and the imprisoned, the poor and the rich, with those whose faith is strong and those who live in doubt. Frank will also be drawn into social conditions he won't be able to control. Through all the highs and lows, he must offer God's grace to humanity by setting its sights on the Kingdom and its fullness. Through this he will develop a healthy self-understanding, a generous spirit, and a sense of humour, laughing at himself and at the absurdities of the human world: traits which are the hallmarks of greatness and excellence.

Grace will be required not only to dispose Frank to pray, but also to aid him in determining what to pray for. He will not always know what he should pray for. There will be certain needs for him to pray for such as his salvation, his resistance to temptation, his practice of virtue, and yet there will also be this constant need for Frank to find light in the guidance of the Spirit, for him to know the kind of help to give to others that is in accordance with God's will. This conformity is implied in every prayer and Frank must ask for nothing unless it is strictly in accordance with Divine Providence. From this energy Frank will then pray for others to have good health, and the worldly and temporal goods needed to live well, and also mental health and moral guidance, and every other accomplishment that is a means of serving God. And there will always be the evils of the world which Frank should pray to escape, and the penalties for his sins, the dangers of temptation, and every manner of physical or spiritual affliction, which will impede him in God's service.

The use of prayer will offer Frank many advantages. Besides obtaining the gifts and graces that he will need, the act of prayer will elevate his mind and heart to a knowledge and love of all things Divine, as well as a greater confidence in God's works. Indeed, so numerous and so helpful will be these effects of prayer have, that they will compensate Frank, even when his prayerful wish is not granted. Nothing that Frank might obtain in answer to his prayers could exceed in value the familiar converse with God in which prayer consists. Frank also merits by deep prayer a restoration to grace, when he is in sin. He will receive new inspirations for sanctifying grace when the temporal punishments for sin overwhelm him, which will then bring him a forward-looking sense of inner peace.

If Frank's prayers to God are humble, they shall surely pierce the Earth's stratosphere and reach him. By not sacrificing his humility Frank can also be sure that if his conscience remains good, without defect in his conduct, his prayers will be answered. Indeed, he may be humble enough to recommend himself to God, provided that the principal motives of his self confidence are in accordance with God's goodness and the merits of the Christ.

Frank's sincerity will also be a necessary quality for prayer. It would be negligent of Frank to idly ask favour without doing all that is in his power to obtain it, and not to beg for it without really wishing for it, or to do anything inconsistent while praying. It is through earnestness and fervour that Frank is to pray. His earnest prayerful expression is his desire to do what is necessarily God's will. And attention is of the very essence of prayer. Frank's prayer will require that his intelligence apply spiritual concentration. As soon as his concentration ceases, his prayer will cease. To begin praying and then to allow his mind to be distracted will terminate it and thus not reach God. He can only resume when his mind is withdrawn from the distraction.

Frank should be able to foresee his spiritual needs, and recall them as sleeping and waking thoughts and turn them to prayer. In order that he in humility pray, Frank must be in adoration of God for him to then to honour Him. He will use his Catholic imagination to construct a scene appropriate to the subject of his prayer, for example the Garden of Paradise, or the Christ's Passion, the Last Supper, Heaven and Hell, which will help him fixate his attention on the spiritual aspect of his prayer. Thus, when considering sin, especially carnal sin as enslaving the soul, Frank while musing over carnal sin, will be free to imagine in prayer his corrupted body as a load upon his soul, and his earthly life an ever pressure upon his mind.

When Frank might vocally pray, the repetition of certain words, in a set form with the intention of using them in prayer, so long as the intention lasts, and he continues to repeat the form of prayer, with proper reverence in disposition and outward manner, and no thought or external act is a distraction which terminates his intention, then he will even be able to pray in crowded streets, at the movies, at football matches.

As a means of cultivating the habit of praying, Frank will recite on a regular basis the Lord's Prayer, and other familiar prayers, slowly enough for him to take a breath in between the principal words and sentences, so as to have time to think of their meaning, and to feel in his heart the satisfactory emotions. Frank will also take each sentence of prayers as a subject of reflection, not delaying too long on any one of them unless he is immersed in a helpful thought and stopping to reflect on it, and when he has dwelt sufficiently on such a passage, finish the prayer as though a luminant light now glows above him.

Prayer is absolutely necessary for salvation. Without prayer Frank will not be able to resist temptation, nor overcome his guilt when he fails, nor obtain God's grace, nor be able to grow and persevere in it. The obligation to pray will be incumbent on Frank at all times. Without it he will not be able to overcome obstacles or perform his obligations such as charity and pray for others as expected by his Church. As a praying priest Frank will need to consistently apply his mind to the study of Divine things in order that he acquire the correct knowledge of the truths necessary for salvation.

Canon 14 - How Frank can be Holy

The Angel's Chorus:
HOLY IS THE PRIEST WHO DEFEATS DISPAIR,
WHO LABOURS OVER THINGS GOOD AND EVIL,
IF NOT HIM WHO ELSE IS CHOSEN TO CARE?
NOT POLITICIANS FOR THEY ARE WOLY-BOLY.

It will be necessary for Frank, in order to reach a stable balance between the needs of the sacred ministry and the duty of his own sanctification, to understand the thirst of human souls ever anxious over life. His passion as a humble priest will be called by God to bear the burden of sorrowful days and their incendiary fires. Within the mystic field of the Christ the priestly Frank will be the true Minister of God, a devout man, one who is dedicated to prayer, who is absolutely upright and who observes exactly every point of both canon law and intimate counsel. He will also be intrepid. Just as in his present youth he has no fear of duty, so also will he be afraid of no man, neither the powerful ones, nor their plots, nor of his own intimate sufferings. There will be many who live far from the influence of the Catholic Church. Those who ignore it and combat it, even they will admire Frank's work and venerate him. He will be a heroic one who is meek and humble of heart, deeply enlightened, and such a frightful an enemy against the powers of Satan and his darkness; who will resemble his Master in the measure in which a man can resemble the Divine. This is the promise awaiting Frank as priest.

Frank as priest will be the man of God who will bring to souls enlightening truth, conquering love, edifying sanctity. He will show forth in himself the beauty of the God-Man the Christ whom he will represent. He will live a life of heroism, in Catholic perfection as an ornament, as a glory and a halo for all members of the faithful, a life of faith which will help him to discern the dark arts of the enemy, a life of hope which will sustain and strengthen him in his daily struggles, a life of burning and inflaming charity, a life of angelic purity, of sacrifice, of a spirit of poverty, of meekness and of a patience which will remain unmoved and unperturbed under the blows of the most atrocious injuries. It must be all this because Frank as priest will then be raised aloft and be the light of the Christ's example and enlighten God's people and warm them with his fervour.

As a venerable priest Frank will tread sure-footedly on the path of ecclesiastical perfection, ordering his life and behaviour in such a way that in his bearing, his gestures, his walk, his conversations, and in all things, he will show forth nothing that is not holy and which does not waft with the odour of pure sanctity. As the stars are visible after the sun has gone down so will Frank become like the constellations and illuminate the firmament of the world in the absence of the Christ who is sure to come again. He must be a man of such irreproachable behaviour that the world will believe that is like a divine man, a man whose virtue is superior to that of every other being. The exhortation to aspire to perfect manhood is addressed to the priestly ministry, who are called to be the other Christ not only because they have received Divine powers but because priests like the future Frank imitate the works of the Christ and therefore bear in themselves His likeness.

There must be for Frank as big a gap between the life of him as priest and the life of an average honest Catholic, as there is between Heaven and Earth. Only he will be able to instruct the people in the law of God. Hence, he must avoid not only serious sins but even the slightest sin, because in them such faults would be mortally serious. Should Frank ever become lacking in the Christ like holiness of his life and purity of habits, he will be lacking in everything. Frank when rich in sanctity will work wonders for the salvation of God's people. His developed unblemished living habits, which are the greatest glory of the Christ's priesthood and the ornament which makes it honoured in the eyes of the world, will thrive and shine forth when he is ordained. He will then be further holy, convinced that it is impossible to be a good priest without perfect holiness.

He will need set apart every day a certain time for meditating on the eternal truth because, as he will work in the midst of the world's seductions, he must be wary lest the snares of the infernal enemy, Satan, be hidden even in the exercise of his ministry. He must meditate so that with renewed vigour his mind and heart will resist the enticements of evil and draw from eternal truth those lights which are necessary in the exercise of his extremely difficult ministry in the care of souls. He must also follow up his meditation by reading books of devotion and above all the divinely-inspired Books of Holy Scripture which are necessary if he is to preach the word of God in a worthy manner. He will regularly examine his conscience as a means of acquiring deeper Catholic virtues. At the end of his day Frank must examine himself and ask judgment of his conscience. He should be a diligent self-examiner in order to know himself and see how and in what manner he has carried out his duties. He should present himself before his conscience as he would before a tribunal and therefore openly weep over his sins.

Frank will also face the inevitable feeling that the labours of his vocation given to him by God to cultivate will appear fruitless, especially in the face of religious indifference spreading out and surrounding him. Only in retreat will there be the means for Frank to get away from the miseries of his priestly life, to help him grow in those virtues which the Christ expects of him. The holy and pure life required of Frank will be sufficient proof for his need for regular spiritual retreating. Regular retreats will be absolutely necessary for Frank's progress in perfection, for renewing in him the flame of zeal for God's service and the good of souls, and for developing within himself a more illuminative and unifying life. In this way he will regularly reawaken his clerical conscience and excite his spiritual mind to the virtues which are the ornaments of an ordained minister of God. The divine fire will be enkindled when he meditates on Heavenly things, and in recollection of his vows and in solitude the Christ will make his voice clearly heard.

Frank's priestly life will be one of great sacrifice. He will work in times when the priest's lot is despised, hated and persecuted. But a comforting thought is that from the spirit of sacrifice, there derives virtue which will frighten all who do not understand the secret of it, and which will strike them with amazement. It is quite possible that Frank, in order to procure the salvation of souls, will run the risk of losing his health and shortening his life. If this does happen Frank will die in glory from labouring as the Christ did when he suffered and died for all of humanity on the Cross. His fight for truth will involve embracing the enemies of the Christ and his Church. He will have a great compassion for all who suffer, recommending them to the Divine mercy. It is a most holy law to defend what is true, just and right, and to detest what is false unjust and evil. It will be his duty to abound in mercy and pardon towards the depraved, in imitation of the Christ who always prayed for his transgressors.

And moved by the spirit of zeal for the glory of God and the salvation of souls Frank will never be afraid of weariness, nor fearful of danger, and not indulge himself in comforts, knowing no rest, nor will he trouble about rewards. Though contradicted and persecuted he will not lose heart, because he knows that the heritage of the Church is the hatred of the gloomy, and the greater obstacles he encounters the more will he have a burning desire to show himself to people as a true Minister of God in everything, in tribulations, in hardships, in distresses, in labours, in sleepless nights, in honour and dishonour. His time will require courage and call for huge sacrifices. He must be strong in the war against the eternal enemy of good.

As priest Frank must always announce the truth. He must never concede to false prophets like Stukeley the Hermit of Granville near where Frank

66

lives, who are under the fatal illusion of winning over erring souls. These people are making a serious mistake and run the risk of losing their own souls. Their foolishness, when it pleases them to fool those who believe them, is the false virtue of the true God over which Frank and his Church will gain victory. Truth is one and indivisible, lasts for all eternity and is not subject to the vagaries of outspoken people in their times. The Christ is the same, yesterday, today and down the future centuries.

When preaching Frank must speak with that gravity which will ensure that his words, his bearing and his way of working arouses love, wins authority and excites reverence, because the very reasons which oblige him to be holy make it a duty for him to show it by his outward acts, in order to teach all those with whom he makes contact. A composed and dignified exterior will win for Frank many souls. Nothing inspires greater confidence than a priest who, never forgetting the dignity of his state, demonstrates in every situation his divinely inspired gravity, so powerful that it attracts and wins universal homage.

His gravity is superior to all in the world, and which commands respect and veneration for him. He will not, therefore, give ear to worldly innovations whose profane maxims influence minds with arguments at variance with the teaching of the Church. A priestly gravity condemns fickleness of thought, which leads people into contemptuously refusing to listen to the teaching and experience of wise men such as Frank, they who are seduced by foolish arguments, and the schools of modern teaching which will bring them to inevitable ruin. And yet there will be times when Frank, inspired by the Christ, will be able to laugh at the world as it is.

Frank's gravity will make Frank love the yoke of self discipline, the only means of him avoiding the evil of doubting Church authority, and which will help him maintain a resolute love of good. Frank must never forget that priestly gravity and propriety will characterize his ministry. Great is

Frank's priestly dignity, but even greater will be his ruin if he is not faithful to his duties, because the corruption of the superlatively good, the Catholic priest, is certainly a very frightful thing.

The minds of Frank's sheep must be enlightened by the continuous preaching of the truth, contradicting errors efficaciously with true and sound theological and philosophical principles. It will be even more necessary that Frank as priest inculcate in his flock's minds the moral teachings of the Christ so that each member may learn to restrain passions, to repress pride, to live in subjection to authority, to love justice, to exercise charity towards all, to lessen bitter social inequalities, to detach their hearts from unnecessary worldly goods, to live happily in the circumstances arranged by Providence and, by reorganizing their lives according to the holy laws of Catholicism, and to aspire to a future life with the hope of eternal reward.

He will know how to adapt the Catholic spirit to the new needs created by the material evolution of contemporary society, knowing that the Church has never betrayed the interests of the people with compromising alliances, that the true friends of the people are neither revolutionists nor innovators but traditionalists and that the Christ never tolerated mistaken convictions in those who were misled no matter how sincere they seemed. The Christ never inspired the humble with rebellious sentiments, never enticed the suffering with the vision of an illusory equality nor ever promised an earthly kingdom in which suffering would be banished. He came into the world so that all people might have peace and happiness in time and eternity, but only on condition that they accept his teaching, practice virtue and listen to the true teachings of his Church.

Canon 15 - The skills of Apologetics

The Angel's Chorus:
WHAT FRANK SAYS THE CHURCH MUST ENFORCE,
ELSE THERE'LL BE TROUBLE IN THE LOW RANKS,
THE TRINITY OFFERS FAITH A THREE MAIN COURSE,
UNLESS PROPERLY CONSUMED THERE WILL BE ROT.

Frank as priest must develop the skills needed to defend his faith. He will learn to exercise a verbal and sometime written defence against attack against his faith, and to disprove false accusations. There is scarcely a dogma, scarcely a ritual or disciplinary institution of the Church which has not had hostile criticism, and which needs to be vindicated by proper apologetics. This, despite the Catholic Faith being so perfect, for it exactly mirrors the perfection of the Christ. Sadly, answers are ever needed to counterattack the attacks of various kinds upon the credentials of the Catholic religion. Apologies must be written and rewritten to vindicate the Catholic faith, which has unjustly been called into question or held up to disbelief and ridicule since its inception.

Frank will need to feel secure in knowing that Catholic Apology is par excellence, combining in one well-rounded system all the arguments and considerations needed. Apologetics is the most comprehensive and scientific vindication of the Catholic belief, in which the calm, impersonal presentation of underlying principles is of paramount importance. It addresses itself not to the hostile opponent for the purpose of refutation, but rather to the inquiring mind by way of information. Its aim is to give a rational presentation of the claims which the Christ's revealed teaching has on every absorbent mind. It seeks to lead the inquirer after truth to recognize, first, the reasonableness and trustworthiness of the Revelation of the Christ as realized in the Catholic Church, and secondly, the corresponding obligation of accepting it. The moral certitude of faith shows that the credentials of the Catholic religion amply suffice to vindicate the act of faith as a rational act, and to discredit the estrangement of the sceptic and unbeliever as unwarranted and culpable.

Frank must always ask himself why the whole human race isn't Catholic. After all it is the one and true religion! Apologetics leads the outsider to the Catholic faith, to the acceptance of the Catholic Church as the divinely authorized organ it preserves, rendering the saving truths as revealed by the Christ. This is the great fundamental dogma on which all other dogmas rest, the one which simply leads to an unconditional faith.

Armed with a deep understanding of the nature of Catholicism, its universality, and humanity's natural capacity to acquire catholic ideas, and knowing the important questions concerning the existence of a divine person, the Creator and Conserver of the world, who dominates humanity, Frank will no doubt help achieve the Church's goal of universal Catholicism. It is free will, a dependence on God, the immortality of the human soul, and the future life with its attendant rewards and punishments which all humans must know.

Then Frank can proceed to establish the fact of Revelation. The chief sources for him to rely on are the Sacred Scriptures. To help him he needs rely on the critical study of the Old and New Testaments by impartial scriptural scholars, and build on the accredited results of their researches, after all he is merely one man of faith among many. The evidence of thoroughly reliable eye-witnesses and their associates who presented the Christ as the long-expected Messiah, the Son of God sent by His Heavenly Father to enlighten and save mankind and found the new kingdom of justice, the unsurpassed beauty of his moral character, the unique, perfect man-God, is all there. The lofty excellence of his moral and religious teaching has no parallel elsewhere. The Christ had come to answer the highest aspirations of the human soul. The Christ

70

wrought miracles and the transcendent miracle of his resurrection, which the Christ foretold. From this all other faiths are easily dismissed.

Frank will also learn how to demonstrate that the true church of the Christ is the Roman Catholic Church. It is from the records of the Apostles and their immediate successors that the institution of the Church is found true, having been endowed with the supreme authority of its founder the Christ, and commissioned in his name to teach and sanctify mankind. By possessing the essential features of visibility, indefectibility, and infallibility and characterized by the distinctive marks of unity, holiness, catholicity, and apostolicity, the Church is simply the truth. When this criterion is applied to the various rival Christian denominations of the present day, they are found to be fully indemnified in the Roman Catholic Church alone. And with the supplementary exposition of the primacy and infallibility of the Pope, and of the rule of faith, the work of Frank as an apologetic should be brought to a fitting close. And yet he will find that the Catholic Church is still not being listened to!

Frank will remain in the Christ's word, and truly be his disciple, and he will know the truth and the truth shall set him free. And then he will lead others to salvation and light through the truth. But realistically Frank will also need to understand that it is not him or his Church which is the problem. It is those who are blinded by their intellect, their free thinking and their resistance to the supernatural who are a problem. Indeed, there are many honest people who do not believe in a God, and who therefore reject Sacred Scripture and Church tradition. But Frank will remind himself that these people are not honest with the Christ and his Church and the arguments of apologetics will always await them.

Catholic theology is there to assist Frank when he talks to doubters about the truth. Already God exists in Frank's understanding. The concept of God had resided as a reality in his mind since his indoctrination from

71

birth. And God is to him a certainty because there cannot be any contradictions to this certainty. To Frank God is that blessed mental germ which can never be eradicated. Since God exists exclusively in his understanding which is therefore his reality and in all possible circumstances, real or fantastic, Frank's anxiety is pacified by his knowing that God's existence is perfect even though God's existence lies beyond Frank's limited understanding. Frank's limitation can only be bridged through his absolute and undying faith in God. But God has also given Frank the ability to imagine Him and while Frank tries awfully hard to imagine Him, he need never doubt His existence.

It is quite logical for Frank to believe that all creatures of the universe were originally created by God as entirely pure and good. They were morally and physically good in the sense that God had endowed them with existence. The goodness of God ensured that everything created by God is entirely good. However, the free choice of the first miscreant, the first rebel, the Devil, to refuse submission to the divine and obey him, has corrupted his good and pure will. It was Satan's choice to disobey and he alone owns it. But he hasn't. He has passed on his evil and malice to all of humanity. This was the beginning and origin of all evil. It is important for Frank to understand that the source of evil is not God. The source comes from the fallen angel Satan.

The consequence of Satan's fall is that he is constantly seeking to destroy all that is good. The powerful Satan, the source of all evil, is a critical explanation for the evil Frank sees in nature. But Frank being human has also asked the question of why God doesn't stop Satan from spreading his evil. Frank yearns to understand that God allows moral evil so that Frank can exist as a creature of free will, who then will choose God over Satan. But there are also the natural evils of death, pestilence, tragedy, disasters, disease etc which God's children, humanity, must deal with. Why does God allow these? In God's eyes these are justices which demand retribution for Satan inspired human evil. Therefore, the moral evils done by humans are punished by what humans can see, that is the natural evils. The human race is bound up as one family, and the evil done by one member merits punishment to all members. The first evil was the disobeying of God done by Adam, got at by the Devil through Eve, which could not go unpunished.

God created temptation to test humans. Therefore, God permits the Devil and his army of fallen angels to prey on all including Frank and on all material things. There will be suffering but God created suffering to be of redemptive value. If Frank can experience the unavoidable suffering of life, he can use the suffering to draw himself closer to God. The Christ of course has shown humanity the way by defeating the Devil, and then dying on the Cross to redeem the world. Frank and humanity will always suffer in trying to emulate the Christ. He must console himself in knowing that by trying, no matter how hard it is, he is drawing ever nearer to God.

Frank already has in place within him an innate desire to fill the emptiness within him. He is after all as a human being no different to other humans in his quest for belonging, security, recognition and understanding, and in his heartfelt desire for a higher goodness. Temporal pleasures and natural love can only be transitory and ultimately unfulfilling. Such powerful and elusive desires are a cry from his soul seeking something which cannot be gratified by the things of this world. Frank's discontent in his heart is the mark of God calling Frank to embrace him.

Canon 16 – The theology of Penance

The Angel's Chorus:
GUILT IS THE CAUSE OF SORROW FOR SINS,
THE CHRIST LOVES SINNERS WHO REPENT,
IT SHOULDN'T BE THAT THE DEVIL WINS,
AND CATHOLIC CONFESSIONALS WERE BUILT.

As soon as Frank hears his first confession he will walk in the footsteps of the Christ, who said of himself to sceptics that he was the son of man and he has the authority to forgive sins on earth. And before the Christ had died and was resurrected into Heaven, he gave his Apostles the authority to forgive sins. When he spoke to them, he breathed on them and gave them the Holy Spirit for them to forgive whose sins are forgiven them, and to them whose sins they retain are retained. And with the Holy Spirit in them the Apostles became the earthly instruments of the Christ's forgiveness.

Frank will learn that through sin his Church itself is regularly wounded; the sign of a continued reconciliation between God and humanity, and within humanity itself. For this reason, faults against the worship of God and offenses against Catholic love are intimately connected. The Church from time and time purifies itself from evil through inducement and renewal. There is no forgiveness of faults without the Church. Reconciliation with the Church and reconciliation with God cannot be separated from one another.

Forgiveness shows itself in spiritual inducement, by which Frank the believer turns away from his previous sinful life, and converts himself with all his heart to God. Frank, who by the remission of his sins liberates himself from his sinful being, and with grace opens up a new life for himself in the Spirit. Spiritual inducement had already begun with Frank's baptism. In baptism the gift of the Spirit was sealed in him.

74

And in life Frank has tried hard to continue his inducement through his ardent faith. Under the direction of the bishop and Frank's baptismal parish priest, the Church offers forgiveness of sins in the name of the Christ, establishing the necessary forms of satisfaction by praying for Frank as sinner. Frank's parish priest had done penance through confession with him, so as to absolve him of his sins and to pronounce his full belonging to his Church community.

Frank is taught that spiritual inducement, a free-willed turning away from sin and toward God, presupposes an awareness that sin is outside of and contrary to salvation. The contemporary crisis of the sacrament of penance is intimately connected with a crisis over what is the sense of sin. It will be necessary for Frank to describe sin as being outside of salvation, as is atheism, as is a refusal to acknowledge God, as is a breaking of a living alliance with God. Sin opposes the revealed will of God and contradicts the law of God and his Commandments. Sin is the refusal to live in the justice that God has given. Sin is falsehood and darkness. It opposes the truth of God, to the Christ, who is the way, the truth, and the life and the root of being human. They who sin do not come into the truth of being human. They who sin do not come into the light but remain in darkness.

Catholic priests know well how to pardon, because they themselves understand how they are most vulnerable and liable to grievously sin. This is why God did not give humans angels to be their doctors, nor send down the angel Gabriel to rule over God's flock of sheep. It is from the gathering of Catholic priests that God has chosen shepherds. From among the sheep God appoints leaders, in order that they may be inclined to pardon their followers and, keeping in mind their own grievous faults, to not set themselves superior to the members of their flock. It is better for sinners to be open with their sins and be absolved, than to hide them and be damned. If sinners conceal and keep their sins within, they will be distressed and choked by sin's horrible biliousness.

Frank as priest will be assured when training in the seminary that confession is not a Church invention devised to secure power over consciences or a means of psychological unburdening for troubled souls. Penance and confession are the ordinary means appointed by the Christ for the remission of sin. Humans were made by God to be free to obey or disobey, but once they have sinned, at any age, they must seek pardon, not on conditions of their own choosing but on those which God has determined, from baptism onwards, embodied in the Church Sacrament of Penance.

But he must also remember that no priest, as an individual man, however pious or theological, has power to forgive sins. This power belongs to God alone. But through the ministration of specially appointed men, such as the future priest Frank, human sin is made to be forgiven. Since God has seen fit to exercise this power by means of the sacrament of Penance, neither the Church nor a priest interferes between the soul and God. The mere telling of one's sins is not sufficient to obtain God's forgiveness through the confessional's dispensation of divine mercy. Without sincere sorrow and purpose of amendment, confession means nothing, the pronouncement of absolution is useless, and the guilt of the sinner is greater than before.

When sins are revealed to the priest in sacramental confession, he is bound to inviolable secrecy. From this obligation the priest cannot be absolved either to save his own life or good name, to save the life of another, to further the ends of human justice, or to avert any public calamity. No human law can compel him to divulge the sins confessed to him, or any oath which he takes as a witness in court. The only possible release from the obligation of secrecy is the permission to speak of the sins given freely and formally by the penitents themselves. Without such permission, the violation of the seal of confession would not only be a grievous sin, but also a sacrilege. It would be contrary to the natural law

76

because it would be an abuse of the penitent's confidence and an injury. It would also violate the Divine law, which, while imposing the obligation to confess, likewise forbids the revelation of that which is confessed.

Frank will be taught that there are many souls in the world in distress, who are anxious and lonely, whose primary need is to find a being to whom they can pour out their feelings misunderstood by the world. They want to tell someone but out of fear do not tell. They wish to tell someone who is strong enough to hear them, but not too strong so as to despise them. It is this weakness of humanity on which the Church speculates. It has been made clear through history that the Church is simply carrying out the mind of the Christ, and that the Church answers to the needs of humans, who morally, are weak and in darkness. There have been Church abuses, but they have been rare compared to the multitudes who have found in the tribunal of Penance a remedy for their anxieties of mind.   And the few inconveniences arising from the perversity of priests, which the Church has met with admirable prudence, should never blind humanity to the great good that Penance at confession has brought, not only to the individual, but to society.

Canon 17 - Frank is in awe of the Holy Catholic Church

The Angel's Chorus:
HOW DOES HUMANITY SURVIVE WITHOUT THE CHURCH?
FRANK IN AWE GRAFTS THE ANSWERS TO HIS PRIDE,
AFTER ALL HUMANITY IS ALWAYS IN THE LURCH,
A PRIEST'S ANXIETIES ARE SCARRED ON HIS BROW.

Frank happily realized by his late teens that his Catholic Church, in communion with all baptized, had been fuelling his vocational fire all along. From his Church he received the Word of God containing the teachings of the law of the Christ. From his Church he received the grace of the sacraments which sustained him on the way. From his Church he learnt the example of holiness, recognizing its model and source in the all-holy Virgin Mary, discerning holiness in the authentic witness of those who lived it.

Because he was a member of the Body whose Head is the Christ, Frank had already contributed to building up the Church by the constancy of his convictions and moral life. The Church increases, grows, and develops through the holiness of her faithful such as Frank, when all attain a unity of the faith and of the knowledge of the Son of God in the fullness of the Christ. And by living with the mind of the Christ, Frank will hasten the coming of the Reign of God, a kingdom of justice, love, and peace. Frank must not however, abandon his earthly tasks, but by being faithful to his master, fulfil them with uprightness, patience, and love.

Frank's Church, the pillar and bulwark of the truth, has received the solemn command of the Christ from the apostles to pronounce loudly the saving truth. To the Church belongs the exclusive right to announce moral principles, including those pertaining to the social order, and to make judgments on any human affairs as required by the fundamental rights of the human person or the salvation of souls.

Human society can be neither well-ordered nor prosperous unless the Church's God given authority to devote itself to work and to care for the good of all is fulfilled. This authority contains in it the virtue of the Church's moral laws and moral orders to humanity which must be obeyed. The Church's authority which requires a stable moral order is derived only from God. Every human is subject to a moral governing authority. There is no authority except from God, and the Catholic laws that exist have been instituted by God. Therefore, anyone who resists Church authority resists what God has appointed, and those who resist will incur judgment and punishment.

The Church makes moral judgments about economic and social matters, when the fundamental rights of people or the salvation of souls requires it. In the moral order she bears a mission distinct from that of political authorities. The Church is concerned with the temporal aspects of the common good because they are ordered to the sovereign good, humanity's ultimate end. The Church strives to inspire right attitudes with respect to earthly goods and in socio-economic relationships.

However, the Magisterium of the Church is not superior to the Word of God, but is its servant. It teaches only what has been handed on to it. At the divine command and with the help of the Holy Spirit, it listens to this devotedly, guards it with dedication and expounds it faithfully. The faithful receive with docility the teachings and directives which their priests have given them.

Frank unfailingly believes that his Church, the bride of the Christ, is holy and catholic, and that she is one and apostolic, is inseparable from belief in God, the Father, the Son, and the Holy Spirit. The Catholic Church is humanity which God gathers in the whole world. She exists in local communities and is made real as a liturgical and a Eucharistic assembly. She draws her life from the word and the Body of the Christ and so she herself becomes a bride for the Christ.

The world was created for the sake of the Church. God created the world for the sake of communion with his divine life, a communion brought about by the gathering of humanity in the Christ, and this gathering is the Church. The Church is the goal of all things, and when God permitted such painful upheavals as the angels fall and human sin, he wanted to give the world his intention of saving humanity, and this intention is the Church.

Frank's Holy Catholic Church receives its perfection through the glory of Heaven, during the time of the Christ's glorious return. Until that day, the Church progresses on her pilgrimage amidst this world's tragedies and God's consolations for them. Here on earth she knows that she is in exile far from the Christ, and she longs for the full coming of the Kingdom, when she will be united in glory with her king. The Church, and through her the world, will not be perfected in glory unless there are great trials.

The Church is essentially visible but is endowed with invisible realities, zealous in action and dedicated to contemplation, present in the world, but as a pilgrim, so constituted that in her the human is directed toward and subordinated to the divine, the visible to the invisible, action to contemplation, and this present world to that city yet to come, the object of its quest. It is in the Church which the Christ fulfils and reveals his own mystery as the purpose of God's plan to unite all things in him. It is because she is united to the Christ as his bride, she is a mystery in her turn. The Church is also a communion of holy men with God, in a love that dare not soil its name. The Church's structure is totally ordered to the holiness of the Christ's members. Its holiness is measured according to the great mystery in which the bride responds with the gift of love to the bridegroom.

The Christ the redeemer has shown himself to be as one with the holy Church which he has taken to himself. The Christ and the Church are one being, and the issue isn't really complicated. Whether the Christ the head or a Church member speak, it is the Christ who speaks. The two are one flesh, as in the conjugal union. The Christ is the distal head, whom the Church calls its bridegroom, and the Church is by the Christ cleaved, calling herself bride of the Christ.

What the soul is to the human body, the Holy Spirit is to the Body of the Christ, which is the Church. To this Spirit of the Christ, as an invisible principle, is to be ascribed the fact that all the parts of the body are joined one with the other and with their exalted distal head. For the whole Spirit of the Christ is in the head, the whole Spirit is in the body, and the whole Spirit is in each of the members. The Holy Spirit has made the Church the temple of the living God.

The Church is the One True Church because her source is the highest exemplar of the mystery of the Trinity of Persons, of one God, the Father and the Son in the Holy Spirit. The Church is one because her founder is the word made flesh, the prince of peace, who reconciled all humanity to God by the cross, restoring the unity of all in one people and one body. The Church is one because her soul is the Holy Spirit, dwelling in those who believe and pervading and ruling over the entire Church, who brings about that wonderful communion of the faithful and joins them together so intimately in the Christ the principle of the Church's unity.

Unfortunately for humanity, there have arisen certain rifts, which the popes have strongly condemned as damnable. Large communities have become separated from full communion with the Catholic Church. The ruptures that have wounded the unity of the Christ's Body, through heresy, apostasy, and rebellion have occurred because of human sin. For where there are sins, there are also divisions, schisms, heresies, and disputes. Where there is virtue, however, there is also harmony and unity, from which arise the one heart and one soul of all believers.

The Church, as a matter of faith, is unfailingly holy. This is because the Christ, the Son of God, who with the Father and the Spirit is hailed as singly holy, loves the Church as his Bride, which in turn freely gives herself to Him as though in the most passionate of all conjugal unions. The Christ has joined his body with hers, having seeded her with the gift of the Holy Spirit for the glory of God. United with the Christ, the Church is sanctified by him and through him and with him she becomes sanctifying. All the activities of the Church are directed, as toward their end, to the sanctification of humanity in the Christ and the glorification of God. The seed of the fullness of the means of salvation was deposited by the Christ into the Church when he joined as one with her as the Church's bridegroom.

Frank's Church burns with an undying love for all of humanity. And this love is the true motive force which enabled the Church to act. The Christ, holy, innocent, and undefiled, knew nothing of sin, but came only to expiate the sins of humanity. The Church, clasping sinners to her bosom, at once holy and always in need of purification, will always follows the path of penance and renewal. All members of the Church, including her ministers, must also acknowledge that they are sinners. In everyone, the weeds of sin will be mixed with the good wheat of the Gospel until the end of time.

The Church is holy despite having chronic sinners in her midst, because she has no other life but the full life of grace which can only make her perfect. If they live her life, her members are sanctified. If they move away from her life, they fall into sins and disorders that prevent the radiation of her sanctity. This is why the Church suffers and does penance for those offenses. Only she has the power to free God's children from sin through the blood of the Christ and the gift of the Holy Spirit.

Canon 18 - The Church's missionary position in the World

The Angel's Chorus:
SELLING THE GOSPEL IS THE CHURCH'S CAUSE,
THE WORLD NEEDS ITS CHARITABLE SERVICES,
DISMISSING IT IS THE FOUNT OF GOD'S WARS,
THE CHURCH TENDS GOD'S BRUISES SWELLING.

Frank's Church is catholic because she has been sent out by the Christ on a mission to save the entire human race from itself. All humanity is called to belong to the new People of God. This calling is to be spread throughout the wide-open world and to all ages so that the design of God's will is fulfilled. God made human nature one in the beginning and has decreed that all his children who are scattered should be gathered together as one. The character of universality which adorns the People of God is a gift from the Christ himself wherein the Catholic Church ceaselessly seeks the return of all humanity and all its goods to it under the Christ the distal head, in the unity of his Spirit.

All who believe in the Christ are called to this catholic unity of the People of God, and in different ways belong in or are accepted to it. The Catholic faithful, and ultimately all of humankind, believers and unbelievers, are called by God's grace to salvation. At present, all who are fully incorporated into the society of the Church are possessed by the Spirit of the Christ, as are all who fully accept the means of salvation given by the Church. And by the bonds constituted by the profession of faith, the sacraments, ecclesiastical government, and communion, they are joined in the visible structure of the Church of the Christ, which rules her through the Supreme Pontiff and the bishops.

The Catholic Church recognizes in all other religions a searching among shadows and images for the God who is unknown yet so near since he gave his life and breath to all things. Thus, the Church considers all goodness and truth found in all religions as a preparation for the Catholic Gospel as given by the Christ who enlightens all people that they may have life before and after death. Even very young children, through no fault of their own, who do not fully know the Gospel of the Christ are yet guided by the Church, so they can seek God with a sincere heart. And, moved by grace given by the Church, children will do God's will as they understand it in their persuaded and informed conscience, because through grace comes the hope of eternal salvation.

And yet very often, deceived by the Evil One, humans have become vain in their reasoning, and have exchanged the truth of God for a lie, and serve the Satan creature rather than the Creator. Therefore, living and dying in this world without God, they are exposed to ultimate despair. To reunite all his children, scattered and led astray by sin, the Father wills to call the whole of humanity together into his Son's Church. The Church is the place where humanity must rediscover its unity and salvation. The Church is the world reconciled. She is the ship which in full sail of the Christ's cross, by the breath of the Holy Spirit, safely navigates the evils of the world.

Having been divinely sent to all nations that she might be the universal sacrament of salvation, in obedience to the command of her founder the Christ, and because it is demanded through her own essential universality, the Church must preach the Gospel to all humanity, as it is her right. The Church therefore must go forth and make disciples of all nations, baptizing them in the name of the Father and of the Son and of the Holy Spirit, teaching them to observe all that the Christ has commanded.

It is from God's love for all humanity that the Catholic Church in every age receives both the obligation and the vigour of her missionary dynamism, for the love of the Christ urges it on. God desires all to come to the knowledge of the truth, willing the salvation of everyone through the knowledge of the truth. Salvation is found in the truth. Those who obey the prompting of the Spirit of truth are already on the way of salvation. But the Church, to whom this truth has been entrusted, must go out to meet their desire, so as to bring them the truth. Because she believes in God's universal plan of salvation, the Church must maintain its missionary position, especially to the poor.

The Church's missionary position also involves a respectful dialogue with those who do not yet accept the Gospel. Non believers can profit from this dialogue by learning to appreciate better those elements of truth and grace which are found among Catholic peoples. In them is the secret presence of God, of which they are manifestly unaware. How else can good unbelievers be good without God?

The Good News must be proclaimed to those who do not know it, in order to consolidate, complete, and raise up the truth and the goodness that God has distributed among men and nations. The Good News is proclaimed to purify them from error and evil, from the confusion of the Devil, for the glory of God and the happiness of humanity.

Frank as priest will ask himself how the people are to believe in the Christ of whom they have never heard. There must be a profound preacher who will tell the truth. Frank then will preach because he is sent by the Christ. No one, no individual and no community, can proclaim the Gospel to themselves. Faith comes only from what is heard. No one can give themselves the mandate and the mission to proclaim the Gospel. The one sent by the Christ does not speak and act on their own authority, but only by virtue of the Christ's authority, as bestowed by him to his Catholic Church.

Entirely dependent on the Christ who gives mission and authority, Frank as missionary will truly be a slave of the Christ, in the image of he who freely took the form of a slave for all humanity. Because the word and grace of which Frank will be a minister is not his own, instead given to him by the Christ for the sake of others, he must also freely become the slave of all humanity.

Thus, the pastoral duty of the Catholic missionary is aimed at seeing to it that the People of God abides in the truth that liberates. To fulfil this service, the Christ endowed the Church's shepherds with the grace of infallibility in matters of faith and morals. The Roman Pontiff, head of the college of bishops, enjoys this infallibility in virtue of his office, as supreme pastor and teacher of all the faithful. He confirms to his brethren in the faith a definitive act of doctrine pertaining to faith or morals and the infallibility promised to the Church. This infallibility is also present in the body of bishops when, together with Peter's successor, they exercise the supreme Magisterium, above all in an Ecumenical Council. When the Church through its supreme Magisterium proposes a doctrine for belief as being divinely revealed, and as the teaching of the Christ, the definitions must be adhered to with the obedience of faith. This infallibility extends as far as Divine Revelation itself.

What is the origin of the world? God created it, answers the Catholic Frank. What is God? Only faith can tell him. What is it to create? He does not know, only God knows. What is the cause of disease, wars, disasters, mass murder? God's anger. Why is God angry? Because humanity succumb to the Devil and sin. What are the remedies which can be applied to these catastrophes? Prayers, sacrifice, processions, offerings, feast days, repentance, confession, guilt, forgiveness, alms-giving, faith. Why does God favour some but not others? The favoured are thankful for what God has done for them. Why are humans wicked? Because human nature is corrupt. What is the cause of this corruption? When the first man was beguiled by the first woman. Who beguiled the first woman? The Devil. Why did God create the Devil for it to pervert humankind? God only knows.

Canon 19 - In the House of God's Chosen

The Angel's Chorus:
SCHOOLING LIKE THIS IS FOR EXCLUSIVE MEN,
WHO ELSE BUT THE BEST IMITATE THE CHRIST?
TOGETHER THEY'LL BE CHURCH KITH AND KEN,
THOSE WHO FAIL ARE ENVIOUS AND DROOLING.

Quite simply a seminary is a school in which priests are trained to be one who works with humanity in imitation of the Christ. A priest is THE representative of the Christ among humans. Frank had left school and entered the seminary in 1963 to begin his mission to carry on the Christ's work for the salvation of souls. In the Christ's name and by his power, he is to teach humanity what it ought to believe and what it ought to do. He is to forgive sins, and offer in sacrifice the Body and Blood of the Christ. Frank's training, therefore, is to be in harmony with this high office and consequently different in many ways from the preparation for secular professions. He must possess not only a liberal education, but also professional knowledge, and moreover, he needs to acquire the manners, personal habits and discipline becoming his calling. The seminary teaches candidates for the priesthood what a priest ought to know and what a priest ought to do.

In the preparatory seminary the aspirant to the priesthood follows the ordinary academic and collegiate course for six years. Frank studies Catholic doctrine, Latin and Greek, rhetoric and elocution, philosophy, theology, Church history, and natural sciences in their relation to religion. He also studies Holy Scripture, apologetics, dogmatics, moral and pastoral theology, liturgy and canon law.

The seminary aims to train Frank's will. In order to restore to the world the reign of the Christ nothing is as necessary as the willing holiness of the clergy. Frank learns to be conspicuous in society for his ability,

88

learning, piety, and his seriousness of life. He devotes his life to study, bears cheerfully the burden of seminary rule, and the theological life. He learns self discipline, humility, unworldliness, love of work and retirement, and fidelity to prayer.

Instructions on Catholic perfection, on the dignity and duties of the priesthood is daily given to Frank in spiritual conferences and readings. These are supplemented by retreats, and by private consultations with his spiritual director. There is a direct intercourse of Frank's soul with God in prayer, meditation, and the reception of the sacraments. The seminary is a nursery of faithful representatives of the Christ for the salvation of humanity. As an ordained priest Frank will go forth as the light of the world and as the salt of the earth.

Frank as a seminarian is a man who is discerning the Lord's call for the Roman Catholic priesthood. By virtue of his baptism, he is to become a member of the priesthood of all believers. He has heard the Christ speaking to him and calling him to a fuller participation in the priesthood. His seminarian life is a life nurtured by a deep interior life of prayer and sound piety, filial devotion to the Blessed Virgin Mary, and a profound love for the universal and the local Church. He is further nourished through a rigorous intellectual formation in a faithful and loving obedience to the Magisterium and the sacred truths entrusted to the Church. The seminary provides an environment in which Frank will become a committed disciple of the Christ, to respond to God's call to the celibate life, so that he wholeheartedly and selflessly strives to save the world.

Frank as seminarian lives in a fraternal community. He prays with other seminarians, working together, taking meals together, and studying together. The seminary is a place where the individual Frank discerns what the Christ is asking of him. During his training Frank will bond with this fraternity and become loyal to the fraternity under the auspices of the Catholic Church. As a Catholic priest Frank will belong to a fraternity who is exclusive when sharing in and spreading forth the Christ's words. The close family atmosphere of the seminary acts as a means for Frank to grow in the Catholic virtue of humility, the indispensable spiritual tool of Frank's future priestly work. And he shall not speak ill of another priest. He shall protect the priesthood in difficult times. He shall remain silent when called by the Church to do so.

And after six years of mental and moral training in retirement from the world, and in the society of fellow students animated by the same purpose and striving after the same ideals, Frank is to be deemed worthy of receiving the honour of bearing the earthly burden of the priesthood. He is to become as though an educated Catholic ambassador, celibate, humble, pious; armed with the spiritual means to live and to work in a very troubled humanity as imitator of the perfect Christ.

And five years into his training Frank went into crisis and broke down.

Part 2

The theological fall of Frank O'Connor

Canon 20 - And Madness Hatches Plenty for the Ensuing time of His Discord

The Demon's Chorus:
IT IS FOR US TO LOOK INTO FRANK'S WEAK MIND,
THE FAMOUS SIX THE RADIO SPEAKS OF,
THOUGH WE ARE SIX WE ARE ONE OF A KIND,
TO THE TRINITY WE ARE A RIDICULOUS FIT.

It was during his mental breakdown, over the period of about six months, that Frank believed a gang of demons were operating in the basement room of the seminary and they were assailing him using a telex machine to send messages to his mind. Within those messages Frank came to learn about them and why they were tormenting him. At night to help him sleep Frank had listened to a transistor radio sitting on a small table beside his bed. And in his unconscious, he heard incomprehensible words which were sometimes supported by strange music. Within these words Frank heard a demon name repeated over and over like a rapid firing chattering machine. Ah the telex machine! This was how they first introduced themselves. There were three demon leaders Mr Sheen, Deep Heat and Brylcream as well as three demon helpers Bex, Ford Pills, and Solvol. They told Frank that they lived in the attic above and they travelled the world by radio signal. Sometimes they assumed human form and went about in the streets talking to people as though they were acquaintances and doing things like shopping and playing sport in the local park.

Mr Sheen was the leader of the demon gang. He was the principal who worked the telex machine. He described himself in Frank's disturbed mind as a grotesque devil with a long red beard, giant red hands, and flat-iron feet. His urine and faeces were never expelled from his body. Instead the waste circulated through his arteries and hollow bones. He told Frank that he looks like a monsignor who used to visit Frank's

92

parish. In working the telex machine Mr Sheen never held back his verbal abuse of Frank. Using the vilest of words and the machine Mr Sheen would imprint on Frank's brain his cruellest smiles. He never told Frank what the telex machine was actually used for.

The second demon in charge after Mr Sheen was Deep Heat who was the translator of the telex machine rhythms. However, the translations made no sense to Frank. They might as well have been triple-speak. To assist Frank the demon saw that he was brain fed the image of a serrated icicle, sharp and deadly, poised to pierce Frank's brain at any moment. He taunted Frank and Frank cowered. Frank vividly recalled his intimacies with his parish priest whenever Deep Heat got hold of him. Deep Heat also told Frank that he never presses the buttons on the telex machine, but he could if he wanted to.

The third important demon Brylcream looked in Frank's mind like a ragged Bishop's mitre whose entire mouth was the main seam and whose eyes sat atop. There was nothing else of him. He was the best liar of the demon gang. He would tell Frank the truth as though God was speaking to him. He insisted that the Pope was as infallible as he. The telex machine was Frank himself. His jokes were obscene and his sarcasm was the worst. And everything said to him was telex said, or might have been, or wasn't. Sometimes Brylcream ran a magnet through Frank's mind and dragged away all his 'good' thoughts.

At certain times, day or night, Frank would hear of a demon called Bex. She was a demon 'she' who said that Frank was her talisman. She would wait outside the attic's door and as soon as Frank fell into a day-dream he would see her run up and down the stairs leading to the attic in a fitful frenzy wearing a long flowing white wedding dress, and never once did she fall. When Frank stopped dreaming, she would then go back through the attic door gently closing it, before returning to her weaving of shredded human flesh into what she would call her 'God Dolls'. Frank actually only heard from her while he was still going to mass, when, during the moments when the priest was performing the sacraments of the Eucharist, she'd simply telex 'sorrow' over and over again.

Ford Pills, also a female demon, went away a lot. Mostly to the outside of the seminary's grounds to converse with other demons waiting to get inside the seminary. She wasn't hesitant in consorting with the male demons she fancied. But sometimes she liked a particular female one. Frank saw her presence in his brain images when he least expected to. Especially when he was eating with his fellow seminarians. And then he would vomit his meal at the sight of her gigantic swollen genitals pressed against the windows of the eating hall. When she got the chance, she would telex him she was a Marilyn and that she only wanted him. And each time Mr Sheen would suddenly appear behind her and clasp her genitals with his red right hand and escort her to her cot before things went any further.

Solvol was the mute demon of the gang. Demon gangs usually have one. But what he lacked in speech, except when Deep Heat decided to translate him and turn them into brain words for Frank to try and interpret, Solvol made up in dynamic demonstrations. He was a contortionist extraordinaire, in that he could turn himself inside out, or make his head poke out of his anus or for a joke he would simply poke out his tongue. Not only that, Solvol would melt himself down to a red jelly and then reanimate himself in a perfect likeness of Frank. This annoyed Frank so much that he would pound his pillow until it was a mess.

To affirm their power, in every rem sleep, through what the Demons call mind-filling, Frank is naked and wandering disorientated around an empty church, the spaces filled with oppressive heat, the air putrid and suffocating, the surrounding windows stained with the rotting carcases of saints, and standing naked before a tabernacle the Eucharist host's

94

molten rays splash blood over his body; and then they awaken him, his nostrils snotty, his head aching, his body covered in a hot and clammy sweat, and with a sewer taste in his mouth, before the Demons would lullaby Frank back into a deeper sleep. Frank did not know whether this recurring dream was the cause of these physical discomforts or the other way around. His fellow seminarians and teachers could not help him. They feared he was possessed by demons and there was talk of exorcisms.

Somehow by means of the operation of the telex machine and Solvol's influence, Frank would experience a kind of tack-headedness whereby a singular thought would occupy him for hours, and he could not rid it no matter how much he tried by thinking about other things. And as these unruly thoughts became more tack-headed Frank felt that his head was flattening and that his neck was constricting and he struggled to breath. Very often these troubled thoughts concerned the veracity of Catholic truth.

During his madness Frank's leg would involuntarily cramp. It was as though his calf was talking directly to Frank's mind in such a way that his hopping and jumping was irrelevant. It was only when Frank quietly spoke to his calf that the cramp would cease. But relief only came when Frank found the right words, and only when his tongue hadn't affixed itself to the roof of his mouth.

His whole body felt at times as though it were shrink-wrapped restricting his blood circulation and physical movements. He felt he was going to die and screamed for Mr Sheen to stop it. His stomach felt as though the lining was being peeled off and made raw. When his fellow priests were feeding him, he never kept the food down.

His mind would expand and contract to the rhythm of his pumping heart, distorting his thoughts toward the Christ in such a way that he laughed in an uncontrollable way and spoke words which could only be blasphemous. His perceptions of all things the Christ became distorted and out of all proportion by converting the sayings of the Bible into a joke book. Frank's libellous thoughts courted excommunication and in his panic Frank became catatonic. Mr Sheen messaged Frank that the unrealistic pressure of being the perfect 'Christ-Priest' was getting to him.

And while Brylcream was sucking the life out of Frank's brain another demon, usually unannounced, would lead the sucker astray and force into Frank's mind a new train of thought different to where the sucker wanted him like to be, and the two of them would be laughing at Frank through each ear giving him a temporary state of high-pitched tinnitus.

Frank, thought himself mad, but he was conscious enough of the mental impregnations made by these demons to at times rebel against them, expressing his violent indignation towards their infiltrations and mockery. He would, from a state of calm, suddenly jump up from his sitting chair, and yell profanities at the spartan walls of his room, twisting around and pointing, his face contorted with anger. And while in the act of his admonishments these tormenting demons then contrived to push a thin thread of seminal fluid through his back diagonally in the direction of his vital organs. His bladder would suddenly give him the sensation of being full. And then his blood vessels began to feel as though coursing through them was flammable gas causing such hot sensations throughout his body. Then Mr Sheen would step in and with the push of a few buttons on the telex machine cause in Frank's head a horrible explosion. Frank's bouts of resentment quickly subsided, returning him as impotent prey to these demons ready to mercilessly scorn and ridicule him again and again.

After these initial introductions Frank's demons began to regularly conference in his head through a process the demons call mind-speech.

96

The demons had fully impregnated Frank's mind through the presence of magnetic fluids flowing in Frank's brain, its rhythms randomly altered by the telex machine. It was time to disorientate Frank's Catholic thinking. Frank does not hear what they say to him as such. Rather a static conveyance of demon-speak emerged, which said to Frank that these may or may not be his own distorted thoughts. It was talk in his brain affected by means of these demon telecommunications. And so, through this mind speech Frank heard for the first time about his free-willing need to disbelieve in the Lord his God with all his heart, with all his essence, and to expel the phantom out of his mind.

From the rhythms of the telex machine static Frank heard a droll pitch, presuming it was Brylcream, telling him in lucid mind-speech that there is no god before him, but if he must make some crude graven image of a god, make it of himself but in mockery, or in the likeness of something nature presents. Ignorance of his weaknesses is the principle explanation of his moral deviations. His duty toward himself is to believe in himself and to bear witness to his personal demons. To think of himself in relation to what is around him. In this way he will never feel alone even when he is lonely. Frank has read and heard a lot of words, and now comes the time to better use them.

But not always was it Brylcream who mind-spoke to him. Bex would come in between Brylcream's messaging and speak elsewhere in Frank's mind. This was as usual, when Frank was still attending mass. She told him that to permanently doubt his faith allowed him to firstly disregard and then ultimately leave his Church. Frank is actually free to stop believing, and knowing this will help him accept his repressed objections connected to his Catholic faith. He can then overcome an anxiety perpetually aroused by his faith's deliberate emphasis on punishment. On having given doubt its full measure Frank is free to find spiritual enlightenment in the real world, not the supernatural Catholic world.

When Frank cried on hearing this his fellow priests believed he was being healed.

During this time Mr Sheen would push the other demons aside and jump straight into Frank's cerebral cortex. He'd tell Frank, through the mechanism exclusive to it called mooning, the lifting into Frank's brain an idea which then floats and undulates in his intellect for hours dismissing all others; the idea that by building incredulity, alluded to by the demon Bex, Frank need not bother with the awkwardness of Catholic revealed truth, for he has the strength to refuse to assent to it. Frank's free thinking is the obstinate denial of the so-called truth which can only be revealed through blind faith. And to harden the point Ford Pill's seductive mind-speaking was enough to interrupt Mr Sheen's mooning by calling for Frank's total repudiation of his Catholic faith, after all his parish priest has already done it, and to dismiss the Christ's authority, which his parish priest had also done.

Canon 21 - On Punching out of a Papier Mache box with no Sides

The Demon's Chorus:
BELIEF IN THE IMPOSSIBLE IS MAD TO BEHOLD,
THAT DEMONS ARE UNLIKELY IS A MOOT POINT,
UNBELIEF MEANS LEAVING THE CATHOLIC FOLD,
FRANK MIGHT THINK OF IT AS A GREAT RELIEF.

In Frank's new thought making, telexed in mind-speak by his demons, it is God who cannot reveal himself because he does not exist outside of the imagination, freeing Frank to absorb the more realistic divinity of his natural surrounds through his own powers. A non-existent God cannot give him the capacity to love Him, nor in return for his conformity have the Ten Commandments heal him. Hope is the fraught expectation from prayer of a divine blessing sent from Heaven. Frank need never fear offending an impotent God-image. He is at rest now, dreaming, not sleeping.

To make a laugh into a dissenting idea, Frank's demons telex that he must seek his personal removal from God, and they are there to help. They telex that the Church's theological trickery is in contrast to Frank's innate sense of goodness and justice, for he need only to be faithful to his self-esteem above all else. Frank's belief system is 'pushing up the quicksilver' now. He'll rely upon his own capacities, for there is neither Godly almighty power nor mercy. Frank need only forgive himself when his conscience asks for it.

To adore a nonexistent God is to acknowledge mental illness Frank's demons exhort in unison. And Frank gets the irony. To adore such a God is to praise and exalt something human made, which can only crush and humiliate Frank's spirit, imprisoning him, preventing him from looking within himself, and being free from the slavery of the idolatry of an imaginary phantom. To   repeat the same 'god' over and over again in the hope of a different outcome is surely a reliable sign of madness! Mr Sheen was slowly lengthening Frank's brain.

Through a kind of practical spirituality Frank's needs and aspirations are logically related to space and time. His life encounters will teach him the most. His senses are his guide. He is truly an end to himself, and the sole maker, with supreme control, of his own destiny and the writer of his own history. Catholicism has been thwarting Frank's confidence and self esteem by creating a hope for a future life after death, by first deceiving him, and then enslaving him to a theology of punishment, repentance and reward. His brain was lengthening even more.

Since it needs the existence of God, Catholicism is anathema to the nature of existence. What humans naturally do Catholicism has systemised and taken possession. The consequences of this offense can only be significantly diminished through the virtue of Frank's intentions and circumstances. Solvol, through his mute talent of thought bursting, tells Frank that as a non believer he must have nothing to do with the existence of a Catholicism thoroughly corrupted by its promulgators. There is no dignity in lifelong repentance and redemption. He will learn to be careful about his in productive living, and to not present his experiences falsely, nor stumble too hard when his ethical, moral, or social life is challenged; all aspects of the true nature of his finite human life.

The demons continue their mind-speaking by telexing that Frank's self-reliance is based on the true conception of human autonomy, anathema to the Catholic dogma of utter dependence on God. The Catholic Church champions itself as the divine gift for humanity's greatest fear, that of emptiness, knowing that humans will do anything to avoid it. Better to be high on the drug of god than be high on the devil of drugs the demons mind-speak in piercing unison. To acknowledge self-reliance fosters the dignity of human beings, since such dignity is grounded and brought to perfection without a God.

The desire for no God is written on the mind, for no baby is born thinking of God. Humans have merely created God in their image. And when children move from childhood fairy tales there is one adult fairy tale awaiting them; and by now adults, in the thick of their lives, have no means of driving the imaginary God out of their minds. The demons scoff. There are cures for their mind-speaking! Only from his experiences will Frank find fleeting happiness God loving humans never stop searching for.

Frank's Demons in conference telex that throughout history down to the present day, humans have given expression to their naive quest for a God in their Catholic beliefs and behaviour: in their prayers, sacrifices, rituals, meditations, and so forth. These forms of Catholic expression, despite the ambiguities they often bring with them, are made universal by the Church causing its followers to mistake rules for the spiritual, and vice-vera. Bryclream knows, for even Buddhists have their demons.

The demons confer that it is for Frank to reject his intimate and vital bond with the Catholic God. There is evil in the relationship between the Church and natural curiosity; in the cares and riches of the Catholic Church; it's many vaticans (demon-slang for scandals); in currents of theological thought hostile to reason; in the unconditional need to believe: in the fraudulence that Catholic myth has built. The demons know well Frank's birth enemy.

Frank is not accountable to a human imagined God whose punishments are meted out by the morally superior through the evil sacrament of penance. The demon Solvol jumps in with deeper thought bursting, to telex that nature and the universe are greatly to be praised, but in awe-full respect. Great is their power and presence and which is without measure. And Frank, so small a part in this phenomenon, though clothed with mortality and bearing the evidence of suffering is still proof that he can withstand adversity. Despite everything, Frank, though a speck of dust in the atmosphere, desires to learn. By nature's being it encourages him to delight in its presence, for nature has made him for himself, that his heart be restless until it finally rests in nature.

The Demons in conference telex Frank that a God, created in the human image and called by god- proclaimers to know and love him, is sought through so called ontological proofs, not in the sense of proofs and re-proofs as in the natural sciences, but rather in the sense of using dismissive and convincing arguments, reliant purely upon faith and hope, which cause humans to learn nothing about the word truth.

For what can be known about this God is bewildering to those who do not believe, because the mythical God has shown nothing of itself to them, unlike demons. Ever since the beginning of the human created sense of time this God's invisible nature, namely, its eternal power and deity, has mistakenly been perceived in the things that humans experience. Invoking God as the explanation for everything is lazy mindedness. Thank God. God willing. God's plan. Try us instead they say. Our complex ways are far more interesting.

In asking of the savage beauty of the earth, of the sea, of the climate distending and diffusing itself, the beauty of the sky, ask of all these realities and see how they are beautiful, for the experience is no different to that of Frank's inner demons. Their terrible beauty is a phenomenon which perpetually changes. In the infinite and timeless universe, everything is made and unmade, for in themselves there is perpetual change. No God will ever change, but have faith Frank they say, because demons are ever changing.

In another conference they telex Frank that the human world which Frank lives in, will never agree on an understanding of their first principle of being, nor their final end, and it would be better for him to participate in every way his being, knowing that it will end on earth bar the memory of him. Thus, in complex ways, there exists Frank's unique reality which is his cause and in this cause is the end of his life; a demon reality they call 'existence'.

Then Frank's atheo-poetics, his thoughts in nature, facilitate in him the existence of a personal and individual self. But for Frank to be able to enter into real intimacy with himself, the poetics of nature, by its ever changingness, means he'll confidently self-reveal and reveal to others things about himself that might be interesting, as he has done to his demons, and have the grace to welcome another's differing view of life individually perceived.

These conference events occurred most during Frank's fitful sleep, with the radio on, where the demons could most annoy him through their subliminal dream workings, creating phantoms and imagery to play about in Frank's mind. They held in their possession chimeras of uncouth shapes and various configurations, and by looking steadily into Frank's brain they rendered their perceptions acutely vivid in Frank's dreams. The crafty way these demons gleaned his waking thoughts and made them philosophy, after they had been swing-dancing in Frank's imagination, created in Frank a distressed wonder.

Sometimes Frank thought he was able to discern them but whenever he had detected their manoeuvres, and endeavouring to discover the image of these demons, they'd step back, and elude his search, so that only split-second transient glimpses of them occurred. The demons themselves didn't actually step back but rather if observed they'd be seen thrusting something at Frank's mind vision which blunted his perception, breaking the mental communication between them and him. Often, to make sure Frank would never discover them, the demons presented a six headed truncheon with which to hit Frank's corpus callosum with, so that forgetfulness quickly took place.

And when the seminary authorities took Frank's radio away from him his demons left him. And for all the psychological and theological undertakings in the attempt to rehabilitate Frank, it was too late.

Frank believed in one God,
the Father, the Almighty,
maker of heaven and earth,
of all that is, seen and unseen.
Frank believed one Lord, Jesus Christ,
the only Son of God,
eternally begotten of the Father,
God from God, Light from Light,
True God from true God, begotten, not made,
one in Being with the Father.
Through Him all things were made.
For him and for his salvation,
He came down from heaven: by the
power of the Holy Spirit He was
born of the Virgin Mary,
and became Man.
For Frank's sake He was crucified
under Pontius Pilate;
He suffered, died, and was buried.
On the third day He rose again
in fulfilment of the Scriptures;
He ascended into heaven,
and is seated at the right hand of the
Father. He will come again in glory
to judge the living and the dead,

and His kingdom will have no end.
Frank believed in the Holy Spirit,
the Lord, the Giver of life,
Who proceeds from the Father and the Son.
With the Father and the Son
He is worshiped and glorified.
He has spoken through the prophets.
Frank believed in one, holy, catholic
and apostolic Church.
Frank acknowledged one Baptism
for the forgiveness of sins.
Frank looked for the resurrection of the dead,
and the life of the world to come.
Amen.
Because Frank wanted to believe.
Again.
Frank believed in one God,
the Father, the Almighty,
maker of heaven and earth,
of all that is, seen and unseen.
Frank believed one Lord, Jesus Christ,
the only Son of God,
eternally begotten of the Father,
God from God, Light from Light,
True God from true God, begotten, not made,
one in Being with the Father.
Again.
Frank believed in one God,
the Father, the Almighty,
maker of heaven and earth.
Again.
Frank believed in one God,
the Father, the Almighty.

Again.

And Frank no longer believed.

Bereft he returned to safe suburbia.
Fell he into restless days and nights.
Over many seasons losing his way.
What books he read he couldn't say.
There were illusions and night frights.
That came from a Catholic dystopia.

He struggled with his mental health.
Running with him in his vacant hours.
Lucid sometimes, demented mostly.
His older sister thought him ghostly.
He'd name a saint and pluck flowers.
Stukeley sent him on a poetic journey.

Part 3

Frank's heroic journey as narrated by himself

Canto One

The Demon's Chorus:
HE IS FRANK O'CONNOR AS HE LEAVES,
HIS HOMELESS TIME WILL SOON VANISH,
HE'LL BE A SWAG HEAD WHILE HE GRIEVES,
WHEN HE'S ALONE ON A SPURIOUS SEA.

This fraught journey sidelines my Granville wanderings;
For now, I've no mental solstice, nor identities to claim.
Stukeley and I have parted ways,
My time with him has lost its welcome,
Unsure where I now belong but not with him.
And it is be better then, that I Travel,
Away from a suburban concubinage,
Away from ragged discontent and melancholy,
Away from angels that they may disperse my vagaries.
I'm in the back side of my catholic time.
If I cannot find the hints of suburban ordinariness,
In the street-scapes, where I've been nourishing myself,
I'll dare to find them this way,
In this epic journey to make me into a hero, to me.
And while away, living in the transit of meaning,
I'll mull over my restless condition,
Because I am no longer who I thought I was,
And this is the understanding.

Let my journey begin in a night's cold theme,
In hesitant autumn, before it's passing.
Let it begin in a local graveyard,
For the unwelcoming dead to dispute the truth of their sad intruder.
There's no real greeting from me, I'm not armed, decorated, nor clean,
My sad eyes are aimed too high, too low,

I've no principles that are worthwhile;
And so far I am feeling sorry for myself.
The dead stir beneath my sandshoes:
'Look at our broken bones, no marrow', they say;
'The worms have gotten to know us and rewrite our epitaphs,
While eternity is enveloping us.
Why is he here, this reinvented con? L'allegro masquerading as doom?'
I'll sneak past the poet's café and past the local post office,
And get away from the purging pub.
I'm to follow a shooting star, and the Aurora night will soon be mine,
And I'll hear the loner's ballad floating up from a rocky crag.
Dark waters flush, and flush again, there's a goodnight rhythm to it,
Like no other circadian cycle.
And a contiguous sea is to seduce me, away from my seminary home,
A mocking aside of Terra Australis,
Nullius for ownership, St Pat's new motherland.

Before I wandered, I was a creation of eternal promises,
Blight with sermons, and dicky seminary beats,
Where blends the damned with the forgiven.
For under a cross shade at tabernacles,
There gathered communards of frocked brothers,
In sinner's black suits, and skimpy jumpers.
They who mingle over long sabbaticals,
Who'll worship Saturdays at the races.
No greater a religion for prosperity, in times of doubt and hell-fire.
No greater a congregation of mateship as in a Sunday god-scape.
Uplifted by lore, Ultima Thule, founded barren, dei gratia,
God's power dreamed of by wandrin' apostles.
Once there was martyrdom and struggle,
Then wars and European fanning;
And a Vatican City grew from cubist planning,
Its squatters having never been evicted.

An empty mind is a theologian's mind;
Fan of the Catholic martyr, and a life that is a maze of jagged roads,
Along which are dumped the sheep-flock needy.
Ownership is by moral deeds, and those who reveal such deeds,
Mould their theologies with ritual and romance.
Catholic evangelists got it, and mixed bodily fluids with blessed wafer;
Converts were mustered,
Never to return to their pagan roots left to fallow,
Their new faith sewn into bibles under priestly glares.

What kind of person I dreamt of wasn't there;
The outsider in me I couldn't share.
I must find the Catholic tall poppy, and kill it,
And journey as though in mythic tales, change my scenery and be a hero,
But leave those god-head heroes far behind.
I should think of carers, parents, the volunteers,
Those who suffer, yet carry on in bricks and mortar,
Who live, but never far from tragedy.
Intimates who gather to ritually mourn,
Who clasp stricken loved-ones tight,
While confronting life's savage might, looking for a kinder future.
These intimate stories of helpful mates from out the back of the suburbs,
Of rooms neat, dins of happy little'uns, crimson cheeks and family trees,
And core values which do not change, and each day repeats, and repeats.
Like any home-grown foreigner I'm neither settled, nor certain,
A sexless rollicker, this misfit doesn't fit,
And feelings are lost because of it.
And pretty soon I'll be a sea's biscuit.
Seminary bonding threatened me, for honest bonding is what I craved.
I've no imagination for happiness,
Just pidgin thought born from original sin,
And no solid grace for day to day living,
For I merely depend on what I think,

And I am a second-hand personality,
From walking in the Christ-man's sandals.
I can't leap from the surf to betting rings,
Nor make juiced cars from empty tinnies;
A pack of clothes, bags of lollies, and I'll be going.
Other dark nourishments await me, in caves, on sandy spits, in the scrub,
Places where other malcontents meet.

The secret cavities within the leaden sky,
Fill and empty in ocean mean time.
The starless night will end in mourning,
After I've sailed on mists into the dawn,
After self-doubt, and I'm rocking on the sea's canopy.
I walk towards the gentle moonlit sea,
Beckoning me with unmet pleasures.
And about my mediocrity there is no shame.
Nor for left-handers and their menagerie,
For kettle boilers and letter writers,
Folk and peer folk who like to talk,
Anarchists who like to drink weak tea,
And for the existential who are escaping.

And half self-pitied, and half-deranged, as I head towards the sea,
I've altered my being and become a swag head.
I'd rather that I become a faux poet, and mimic my decorous heroes,
The three Johns,
John.... Shaw....Neilson; John Keats and John Clare.
A swag head, a being akin to Ulysses,
Iron-tipped, ironic, and iron willed.
A mimic of melancholic poets who rise like wit bleached phoenixes,
Urchin disciples of Madame Graffiti, her wisdom writ on railway walls,
Dissenting words and mildly dyslexic.
She is muse to the under-thought, and a statement to be read and re-read.

I liked seeing her wit-drenched words, on concrete,
On white paling fences.

I a swag head, this benumbed blanket, a distracted Anglo-Celt,
Skulking amidst a grey backed wilderness,
Written of by apologetic historians atoning for struggles and misery,
Founding their guilt in bibliographies,
Finding peace in a critical mind's wreckage,
And in the cravings of bereaved descendants.
My thoughts are by now subversive,
And redeemed I'll be wrenched out of them.
I a swag head, from reinvention to decay,
Am complicit in my mind's restlessness,
Lambasting my soul; its insignia
Pinned to me as a perforated picayune.
My misery appears mundane, as everyday as a footy scrap,
With bleeding mouth, and ear canal.
All because I'm left alone, a ragged waster, a skittish crone,
Stealing away in the night under cover of descending mists,
Which spread and scowl at me.
And hungry for a long darkness, I believe that the calm sea nearby
Will offer nothing but my reclamation.
I will brood and I am frightened.
I'm like a wreck's ruined skin, its scales the rust of all things.
I've become rotten and wretched, open 24 hours to my disturbances.

I'm on the beach, flat and plain.
I learn of each grain, its manufacture, its lineage and geomorphic strains.
Here's this local beach, it has a name, found on topographical maps,
And spied on from satellites anchored high.
I'll meet with the low latitudes, crossed by strange longitudes,
And after storms, I'll lose myself, and offer my inhabitancy

To the sea's long depths.
The lambent moon above is a street lamp bowed over slattern waves.
I'll work out, and set things straight, I'll mould an image, be a form,
Become a figure for myself to like.
I'm easy dressed in plain slacks, for distress is better met in casuals.
Sail in thrall, upon a sea at large, and I am brave, ironically tested,
With nothing but my diffidence at hand.
From little things little things come!
I'm as fresh as the sea's best skin,
And I recall my new being in strong beat.
I project it, and repeat it slowly,
A swag head, swaaag hed, swaghead
...swag head
Adding a syllable, tone enhanced,
I'm prostrate before the Madonna Moon.
This mountain sea, I'll iron out, my eyes, my hands will do the job,
For I've had enough of limbic strains.
All I need is a seminal break and travel ways unexpected.

The dinghy I've found leaves its scaly moor,
And I pull away from a rutted coast.
And I draw from the coven's frame
A warm pair of Huon pine oars.
I hear soft waves, gently beaching,
Sounding like repeated, heartfelt praise.

Canto Two

The Demon's Chorus:
HE CAN'T YET RISE OUT HIS BODY PIT,
HE LIKES TO REMINISCE ABOUT HIS LIFE,
THE SEA'LL SORT HIM, IN A WEE BIT,
HIS WALTZING MIND THINKS IT'S FREE.

I'm welcomed by a poltergeist sea,
Its mists brewed from out the Tasman,
Its sagacity has powers to alter moods,
Wind initiations which strafe solo sailing.
Imaginations puréed in vapours, non-extant, non sequitur,
On this day eternally known as Good.
A fearful day when crosses are kissed, and blood is spilt,
In intimate death,
Celebrated in chocolate mood, the flavour of sweetened belief.
And on the third day into my crisis the disillusioned Christ fled me.
His flesh, blood and water were rising,
His rags covered in blood freckled moss.
And the resurrecting Christ, chaperoned by mole-skinned Cherubs,
Had gone like a vapour to Heaven,
A bathos spirit smelling of guano.

Inspired by the sea's patterns I reflect on my past,
The lost honesty, the lost grounding, the pained praying at night.
Weeping walls which surround churches,
Are where flowers never grow.
My confessions' sombre dramas in atmospheres of cold indifference,
Were my inviolable exchanges with God.

New swells slap my furloughed boat's bough;
I'll bluff these sea motions with a stare,

And consider each bump a new success.
They speak of a shaky existence,
Confirm that heroes have too much will,
And urge close inspections of past damage.
Let unstable floating work on my mind,
And let new threats come calling on me,
Along with a good old rock dashing.
The air's crisp like ice, hurting hard thinking.
My introspections begin their rage,
And I'll be stood over by melancholy,
In alliance with the sea's warring tactics.

In fantasy, a sweeter taste had come.
I was cradled in the Virgin Mary's arms,
But the Christ's love for me soured,
And still I believed it would return,
After what that priest had done to me.
The ultimate conspiracy, faith, that saw that I be a castaway.
'You are not who you think you are!'
Bark Granville Ruffians to THEIR mums.
And say rebel jurors to the judge, and say the unloved to strangers,
And says an iced donut to its hole.
I'm escaping that disgrace, and smirking like an offensive comedian,
Who's given faith the good old dirty bird.
And says the ho-hum to the buzz, there's truth behind the wildest of lies.
And says a mannequin to its Georgian wig,
And says a dung heap to its mountain,
'You are not who you think you are!'
The passing swells talk the talk.
Sniggerers they likely are!
Fermenting my epileptic thoughts.
The swells know all about untamed wit, deadly on this fractal sea,
Turning spasms into hysterical fits.

Perhaps if reborn, I'll investigate possibilities for something better,
To live 'goody' before the end.
Begin an interest until qualified, work as a plumber, live as a poet,
And defend each role, at least!
Nurture the passion and keenly follow it,
And ignore advice spoken hollow.
I'll find the muse Shaw Neilson had and sing up colours from my depths.
Build rainbows on rainbows to the moon,
'You are not who you think you are!'

My parish priest told me to be vulnerable was good.
First, seek milk from the Virgin's breast, next, be awash with penance,
Attend the finest churchy meets,
But never wander street malls late at night,
And be the good altar boy who imagines a spiritual life.
It was evil to daydream, and climb the peaks of Gondwanaland,
To examine stones of glyphic Egypt,
Seek mysteries in long, low caverns,
And dive undersea to coral graves.
I dared to dream as though inspired, and be the beacon for a 'morrow.
Talk about loneliness in a singles bar!
'You are not who you think you are!'
Yelled old mates from cow-horned sedans.
Their Sheilas said they liked me better:
My shoes were black, my red hair curly,
A slender body vanilla tanned.
Family history is deliberately vague,
Schooling defended against illiteracy,
My older sister read me lyrical poems.
Though my brain is planet sized I need not garnish vegemite sandwiches,
Nor be a Granville Ruffian's cur, who strafe bent roads with knives.
Never any appeal in dealing cigs, nor be a pudding for welfare.
They say that Granville is a hole,

Within, without: Does it matter?
There are others, like Parramatta, Blacktown, and Sylvania Waters,
Who cares about golden roots?
The believer in me I'll try to snuff out, my culture's Alma Mater,
My congregation remain unmoved,
'You are not who you think you are!'

My times with the rosary was said on bended knee just before dinner,
Dadda goosestepped the Catholic way,
As the head of a vinyl topped dinner table.
There were long hot summer days,
Backyard sandpits were dirty and nice,
Chooks were laying scrambled eggs.
Better to play dead inside a fence, than play the dead cat on the road.
Smells of home life spread into the streets paved with rubbish.
Truckies blithely held up traffic,
It was quicker to walk than to overdrive.
Snooker halls were a ruffian's meet,
A place to forget insignificance.
Long billiard cues struck with kryptonite, red balls flew at artistic angles,
Sharp anglers know who they are.
Backs arched over snooker tables, eyes, arms, legs catapult,
As the white ball hits one coloured, straight into its foster home,
Fetched, and put back on its spot,
'You are not who you think you are!'

At a morning calm, a first warming, the sun's rays excite my sternum,
The weather's persistence is welcomed,
With a bow and a servant's gesture.
This is where I think I belong, riding this grey sea's lumps,
And not for the growling bishop, raking across head and folly,
Which suffer from dogma militancy.
I was lonely in grid sermonations, throbbing missals and hefty penance,

117

Except when I'd climb empty silos and spy yonder Blue Mountains,
That leant over urban palates,
The pleats of wilderness.
A place where a God was a grey spare rock, hidden in native grasses,
Not in churches filled with priests with seated arses,
The crowns of seminary legs, which left walking for other pleasures.

On this soup seagulls seek their roost.
I and they eye the floating scraps,
In slow motion, on a sonorous sea.

Canto Three

The Demon's Chorus:
ONCE HE EMPTIED OUT HIS MOCKING SCORN,
AND RAN FROM HIS PARENT'S CHOICES,
IT WAS A TIME FOR HIM TO DULY MOURN,
HE'S BEEN HUMILIATED, LIKE A DUNCE.

Soon whipping winds had come, but they wish me no harm.
They merely reminded me
Of those anxious Catholic days.

To dissent is therapeutic.
Inspired by my parent's blind faith,
I imagined a bright side of purgatory.
And I thought I'd found a proper discourse,
At the last Station of the Cross, tolled by a Trinity of Ghosts,
Arguing with menstruating spirits,
Over whether the Christ had a doubtful gender.
The arguments spilled into wastelands, and into waste-dump streets,
I'd wander them dreaming, gritting my teeth,
The mind gangs never trusted me.

It seems now to me how young rebels got so little from the good news!
My scripture reading looked a duffer!
It could do with some modernist fluffer,
And be sexed up with rambunctious verse.
The last manipulator, a Judas, had left me.
None but demons pull my strings now, daring to challenge the Diceman.
The odds of finding spiritual perfection,
Are longer than praise for the cannibal Pierce,
The other side of the national hero.

119

When I was a learner, I fell awkwardly into years of pimples and pus.
Granville was unaware of what I thought of it,
And what angels should rule it.
Honest Elders and housewives should;
And other oppressed creatures, diminished by their circumstance.
The good suburb folk never disputed me,
When I walked with God bedside me.
Nor did I have fears for their future.
Self-analysis worked on self-esteem in solo séances,
Held as I walked the quiet back streets, talking with God.
I associated words and embraced phantoms
And I looked to my sister like a troubled mental patient,
A bizarre loner mincing,
Keen to muster unqualified voices, Angels, to speak on my behalf.
My spume is what psychoanalysts crave, spume in pubs,
Spume at Catholic masses.
My mildly intellectual brothers followed me,
Embracing me as their hero outsider.
Yet in a good mood I was pert and pleasing,
Filled with Oz rock lore I secretly studied.
I'd speak kindly of rock 'n roll legends,
Who blew out their breath on the big stage.
If I'm disillusioned now, it's profound:
Only dogs keep their promises, for to masters they are bound!
Such was my Catholic anxiety, that goes and comes around.

The sea controls my imaginations.
The weather has metaphorical roles to play.
Suddenly two evening seagulls appear on my dinghy's bow,
Jostling like a pair of drunken monsignors.
And they fight each other with pogo arms,
And jelly fists fly in complex directions.

These old priests had potential, who cared an awful lot.
Dark brothers who lived in speckled light,
Carefree and ready for a suffering life.
These aching stars once happy flesh, now explode in frustration and fly,
Above a coral reef's pure whistling breath,
On this still-aired evening.

A blow to the back of the senses, and these spirits of black comedy
Have fled for some other disturbed sailor.
I'm a parody of spiritual men with no success to speak of,
For the grail of holy achievement is elusive,
There are some who'd rather dismiss it.
The art of lifestyle advertises well, and like a fool I thought not to buy it.
When my Catholic guard was down,
I sought advice from an Elvis pretender,
Who spoke to me when Elvis strolled down my street.

When clarity ripens, and exposits quality,
This is my holy quest, yet it withers at my grasp.

Sailing into another morning glory,
And my time at sea enters days.
And from my skinny chest hangs a convict weight and chain.
A closing fist surrounds my heart.
A growing panic is this dark minstrel's fare.
As discomfort with solitude grows,
I'm like a swami with a case of the gripes.
I'm exiting hours like a trapdoor spider, and I eat like a swallowing frog,
Drinking water like a tap lapping cat.
Binge thinking is my pessimist's indignity,
And as for elusive courage,
It was forged when I was a Granville teen,
By making a pact with the Ruffians, exhaling their holus bolus angst,

To the rhythms of their chest thumping.
They lived near me, over in Muscle streets.
An odd bunch me and them, purging Granville's savage conformity.

Alone or now when silence overwhelms,
I seek relief by throwing myself into the unknown, that is knowable,
By unknowing the known, that is unknowable,
And then knowing the unknown in the knowable.
The friction is serendipitous, and chaos takes centre stage
Directing peerless myopia,
And I'm forced by winds and breezes into stranger directions.

In recurring daydreams I'm sitting alone
Beside Granville's polluted creek,
Spying fish spawning, and walking backwards.
They'd been doing it for awhile,
To the dismay of Scalacumulus the Fish God.
Had I not prayed for the deformed fish below?
In dreams I'd lean over to find the source of the creek
And its strange mutations, to understand the odd way it flows.
From fantasy to myth to fact, the sources of the creek's life cycle
Is lost to progress, and lost in pollutants.
Its solution is left to pop songs sung by Lulu, the song goddess.

And now I, born son of Scalacumulus, fish creator,
Indream arise and dive in.
And like all good fish, swim the stream's beds into long darkness,
Taking chances beneath wide-open constellations,
While searching for the creek's source.
Power derives from clean water,
Through invocations of algae,
Through mediations on fish stares, through gills sucking in air.
I've kicked out the polluters and sat with their children.

122

And through scripture my lore and knowledge pass,
From ancient trees and mountains high to the ears of welcome disciples.
All will hear my plain wisdom and visionary scribes will write it up,
On leaves, on bark, in dots and dashes;
Its veracity will challenge sceptics.
And yet, the more things change, the feeling remains the same.
And time splits theologians, then fools 'em,
And my prophetic words evolve poorly.
Scalacumulus my father,
Had left too many questions that must remain answerless.
Survival is the challenge for prophets like me, the son,
Whose ideas are mortally wounded by deranged fantasies.
Prophets instil precautions through ambiguities,
When the knowable unknown
Is too tempting for their enemies.

Belief inbreeds with superstitions, spruiked through hearsay,
And again, troubled, I withdraw into myself.
My genius for day dreaming derails my desire for a change.
I'll die, as revenge for errors, committed under a lowering lid
Of a sedated orb, that cheers for me this swag head, in my soma,
And so very trippy!
The setting sun's red rays peep through bony clouds,
Manipulating my machinery after another empty day at sea.

Canto Four

The Demon's chorus:
WHEN THE BOY MATURED, HE WAS COY,
THE FUTURE HE SAW WAS PUT TO TRIAL,
EXPECTING NOTHING BUT PRIESTLY JOY,
HIS SMILES WERE TRANSPARENT THEN.

And the sea journey continues, and I'm mesmerised.
What did the Christ say that happened in my mother's womb?
Something occurred in there, it was Original Sin,
Fleetingly faint like an embryo's burp.

And certain genealogies of sloth began with holy men grazing grasses,
Hairy skinned with unruly arses.
Nappies created hip-heaven men!
From them all wisdom depends, bluff is to reason, what fear is to doubt,
Boredom and the way it is handled.
Tell lies long enough and the fiction is believed.
Deeper is the sin, diviner is the grace, and like the mentally ill,
I've yelled for certainty in rules.

I was born,
Over thirteen minutes, and thirty-nine seconds,
God growing my soul while my mother was in pain,
In a Catholic hospital astonished by births from monogamy.
Ecstatic family joy was renounced for my birth's sake.
My parent's Catholic inclinations gave me no choice,
But to live upstanding on the promise of fantasy love.
And they thought me a new Jesus, to defend against the ordinary.
My miracle birth banished an attendant fog outside;
It had lifted when I screamed.
And the showing sun took its peep at my angelic face,

And smiled, its unitary light penetrating me.
My mother's midwife told me this, my only embarrassing love,
Later, when I was thirteen.

And born was I, with a magician's fork protruding,
The pronged symbols of belief, the four quartets of a life ahead:
Believe, pray, repent and die.
My will is absolutely free, if only indecision would step aside!
Damp now sleeps in my stricken chest that came after I was born,
Challenging my adult health.
On these cold nights, I double my skivvies and long johns.
Health limits creep; in old age, in disabilities, and toward death,
Held at bay by athletic elders.
My good health is but wishful thinking.

Sydney's far off coast lifts and drops, lights haughty in the sea fog.
White polar stars rise and fall and fool photographers,
And travellers alike.

I am this smelly swag, who is nervous.
My calling to fulfil my parent's destiny ends with this journey,
And will not have its reprise.
Perhaps I might yet nurture and feed urgent mouths, beget by my seed,
Which I might get to send off, a dozen times or so.
And then chart the bairns' their uncertain courses with advice,
Money and fair warnings, like mum and dad could have done.
The bairns will be educated to the full,
And fly steel winged into adulthood.
My parents are prematurely wrinkled, duty bound, and duty done.
Their catholicity laboured for my cause,
And pleased they used their faith just enough.
And sure their palates lack gourmand,
Women's Weekly recipes haven't tutored them.

And sure they like soapy dramas that retells Testament foibles.
And in their journey of conformity they've kept society on a hum.
They'll be rewarded with caravanning north,
And life membership of the Club.
Obesity hasn't mattered;
And dad goes a bit mental when there's an anniversary,
When he speeds past a violet blue into a sorry black.
Pressures have taken their usual toll, forcing his larrikin humour
To reach into his nether spaces, a Catholic man awfully droll.
He hasn't been alright like Jack, but he's sorting himself out,
With mum's loyalty and patience; and soon, in their vibrant winter
Firm of foot, amid paspalums,
They'll enjoy a pensioner's sojourn in cluster housing, near the coast.
Weedless gardening will suit mum,
And tanked up water tastes better.
Shopping will be by the phone, and aged care will knock three times
Before they enter.
They are the aging revolution, silver romantics, waltzing Matilda,
Breathing exercises and Tai Chi.
Dad will reread his old John Le Carre,
With no harsh words, nor the swearing.
And he'll answer the speaking toilet
With "I'm very well, thank you".

In my night's discomforts I crimp in my formless sleeping bag,
Like an overweight moth in its cocoon,
And my chest cavity thickens with phlegm.
And underneath my itchy scalp fear is my worst creation.
Just leave anxiety until the sunrise and see what happens,
For everything guarantees the weather.

And this sleeper awakes to a tempest brew, farther west.
I smell its sea breath, and feel its chill and squall,
As I drift toward its naked gyre.

Canto Five

The Demon's chorus:
THINK NOT OF HIM AS MENTALLY ILL,
HE'S AN ACREDITED SERIAL FAKER,
THOUGH HE'S NIBBLED ON A BITTER PILL,
HE'S NO WHINGER, HE'S NO FINK.

I fear the storm will be cruel.
And befitting my lowly rank, I muster bravery by calling
With the faintest whisper my imaginary guardian Angel Woo,
To stand beside me when it breaks.
An effigy of my frail self appears;
A lolly stick figure bound with glue,
Will help me stand against this menace.
This storm should get a life and leave loners to their troubles,
Like me here in my plimsoll bubble.
Woo's magic provokes my laughter, a comic jelly, when inspired.
Woo, do your ancients the honour of guiding to safety
A brazen simpleton, who calls himself Frank!

The blackening curtain is closing in, its morbid winds howl for blood.
The fish have scattered, as do gulls and canny dolphins.
It's just me who'll face this garish brute, in my tiny, wooden dinghy.
And lo, the rains and winds in this Tasman Sea soup,
Begin their casting about.
They'll look for ways to toss me far over heaven's backside.
The black is spreading, the splattered sky goes wild,
And I'm clamped to the mast.
My ears I dam with cotton wool from the storm's murderous cries.
My plexus, my thighs I tense, to face tortuous winds
And their thousand lashes.
In a whirlpool's crush stampeding waves slap at me when they pass.

And the winds scream at me;
They will tear me apart.
Lightning stab at me from all directions, and withdraw,
Woo's courage was too much for them.
Peels of thunder roll across the sky roaring at me.
Grey frocked clouds burst open with drenching rains.
And my dinghy rises and falls in the waves' hands
Passing, with the storm's eye, stroking my body, caressing my face,
Trying to cast dear Woo aside.
My skin is rather lemon tough, and my will is as punishing
As the waves that mock me.
And I fight with raw fear, and with general peace,
And with weary hope, and the time feels like a dose
Of imbedded flu and crippling pain.
And the winds and waves batter on, the rains perpendicular,
The thunder raucous, until suddenly the storm weakens;
The dinghy has kept its balance and flops at the storm's back door.
The tempest has passed on by to leave an alarming silence,
As does the clearing sky.
And after untying myself I survey the outcome.
The sighing sky blue sea is flat save for white foam.
The sea green sky is cloudless, the air is beetling thin,
And a thousand gulls arise from the sea spray
And follow the trailing winds.

I've made it without a prayer, the storm hasn't been that bad.
And I'm thankful for Mistress Luck,
And for cherub Woo's sterling help.
Fortune favours the stupid, as it is written on
My sopping forehead.
Sea capers like this add silliness to instability.
And the comedies and mental yanks
That plays with thinking, stimulate difficult questions.

And having survived I sit down and slowly eat,
Speaking kindly to myself,
Hoping one or two good words might escape over the seas,
Into the streets and neighbourhoods,
Then across deserts and mountains,
Into ancient caves where gossip began.
Other people could then tell me I'm not everything to everyone.
They play their part, I play mine, and yet how conscience nags!
Be not selfish, sinner boy, show your class in other ways,
As hungry Lazarus did, who rose again,
And found his death certificate!

Once upon a time, Biblical parables
Had taught me everything about the good life.
And when I lunched with mum at the chippy I always reverently ate,
And chewed slowly, quietly slurping my drink.
This is when I struggled to remember the less fortunate,
As Stukeley the seer told me I should.
I think of this old man now.
A hermit whose hair was translucent white,
Whose face was lined but kindly, whose eyes shone marine bright.
And to his fibro cladded cave, escaped children like me came.
And we heard his fantastic tales, of monster parents turning good.
He told of magic-wand-waving fairies wearing hob-nailed boots
Who could dispel children's fears.
Stukeley's words come back to me now.
'And good children you could be bad if you act up and argue,
Arousing your parent's distress.
You must learn to be preoccupied with the little things you might do.
Your great ideas will mature along with you, and out you go,
Far from Granville, far from the big island,

Maybe as far as Berlin. Have you ever heard of Berlin?
A great city in Europe's belly, which got upset a couple of times,
Making a mess all over the place.
The cleaners conquered and baked the city into a pie,
And afterwards sliced it in two, One East, one West,
And between the pieces a great wall was erected.
So far it is still standing, imposing,
Keeping the slices apart, to see which one runs out of filling.
When you mature you might understand,
The same slices had different crowns.
The divisive wall kept those who felt deprived
From those who had prosperity.
Which slice sees it which way?
And we all share the same problems
With the separated, and the not.
The common good is always equal, in the purblind eyes of its masters.
It is they who promise food for empty tables,
Clothing for exposed backs, shelter and lifelong hope.
And history's masters say it is better to try something and fail,
Than to try nothing at all!'

And here is me drifting in my head sea drifting,
Just scum confetti on a long sea.
Weak, like that scattered storm, yet still am I strong enough to survive.
This journey is an epic, is it not?
A great getaway, to find myself?
Like Stukeley the seer, I'm hiding to expose myself.
Born to die; the romantic cliché,
I know I'll die; nature's touché.
How to live and manage my flaws!
Yet self-praise refers me not, could I be easier to get along with?
I've dreams to keep at my bedside, cushioned by sixties pop songs.
How should I cultivate burdens? With hope?

130

Or leave it to significant others?

Go and rest, you worry bead says a voice inside my brain.
Rest your troubled tousled head, unfurl your swag, your tramping bed,
See what the morrow brings, see what lumps will hit your dinghy.
And whilst I take a shift of sleep the worried moon has gently
Drawn me to an island,
And without a sound I'm grounded on a sandy spit.
And upon waking I see a throbbing neon sign.
It says
Ha Ha Satan's B & B.
NO VACANCIES.
And it flashes over this island beach,
On which I lie, flat aback.
I hear waves roll into me.
Wondrous sounds of the siren sea envelop me, and it soon sends
My worries away across the big pond yonder,
For me to sleep peacefully again.

Canto Six

The Demon's chorus:
TRY HE MUST TO ACT THE PENITENT,
NOW THE DEVIL'S GOT HIS ATTENTION,
THOUGH HE'S DUMB LIKE AN INNOCENT,
HIS OLD SINS ARE ADVANCING NIGH.

The sea breezes listen
While indream I lie in uteri under them.
My bodily systems have shut down,
And my memories mill about,
Take to their corners and then brawl.
I'll do some crying, laugh a little,
I'll let ecstasy fall over me,
While the breezes conduct this peace,
Guided by a watchful moon.
And Ha Ha Satan will await
Until I go into a REM sleep,
And then it will pounce.

'Who are you, given unto me?
Certainly not your material side!
So here you are, on Ha Ha Satan's flat,
Looking a little worse for wear.
Wait, I'll slip into something comfortable.'

And beslacked Ha Ha then sits,
Shirt unbuttoned,
Designer blond tuffs of hair
Gracing its machismo chest.
And in this latest reincarnation
A gold chain adorns its fleshy neck,

And its oily hairpiece is well groomed.
Around its ruddy face, the sores,
Some scabrous, some are weeping;
Ha Ha's face is reminiscent of the fabled ogre.
Its pupils are bright blue, their palate pink,
Fleshy mouth, an aubergine split,
And over it, a pencil thin moustache.
Its crimson body, a clammy cadaver
That swells and shrinks.
Its demeanour and cruel gaze are unsettling.
It looks sick, and the stifling air
Overwhelms my stupefied swag head,
To whom it now gives a serve.

'I am as unwell as I ever was,
Since my good self's elevation
By those weaklings out there,
Demonising me; Me!
As if I have leather wings and filthy nails!
I limp; I am a serpent, a toxic mist,
Yet look at me, I resemble you!
I'm created to be despised and crippled,
But I am unbroken and I still have my days.
I swell again, and my shirt near bursts.
It's all about love's madness,
This diatribe,
And the satisfaction I get from it,
And lucky Frank here is hearing it.
I like myself, for I am equal
To the benign menstruator
Up there in the sky posturing.
I shake my psoriatic fist at the lie.
That white bearded, omni demon

Can't exist without me!
Fawners, sycophants, why do they pray?
What do they see in that Ouija phantom?
A happy life for the immortal soul?
Still they blame me when faith founders.
They who exegete ambiguities;
Ah the neurosis of it all!
And I've NEVER made them do it!
Oh, but I do like contention.
Goodies and baddies who war.
What is faith without its scapegoats?
And really, I am made for this role.
I can get down dirty, all legit like.
And I've got my aficionados,
Ever heard of Black Sabbath?
The Stones gave me their sympathy.
I'm a little precious, I admit.
So are you, for you like talking.'

I'm a dumb Frank who is bound to gawp.
My tongue is looped around itself,
And my heart's a'pounding
Like ten oaken sticks drumming.
I feel Ha Ha engaging me
As though it is really talking to me!

'I live in troubled minds,
I am darkness that swells the brain,
Cleft between skull and membrane,
Through which all seasons travel,
And where dark minds unravel.
If not for me, no incarceration,
If not for me, no retribution,

If not for me, no redemption.
Ignited passions search for me,
And the anger;
Hell's sulphuric rage,
How it overcomes normal beings,
And they become vexatious beasts.
Such vile creatures,
I myself am afraid
For the praying victim on its knees,
Begging for mercy.
You up there!
Yes you, mighty Hombre!
Stop this crime, stop it now!
As you see I swell and sweat.
Ah too late!
The horrible deed is done.
And my swelling recedes, for a time.
Occasionally, I am never needed.
Heroes emerge, and good luck,
I get to take a millisecond off!
I am friend to every soul.
And one word defines our relationship,
My good name that's always spoken
In friendly company, in infant's cots,
In creeds fundamentalists eat
For breakfast, lunch and dinner.
I like that word, it tastes like sinner.'

Ha Ha delivers its diatribe with a lisp,
And smiles over its inbred thoughts.
It could destroy me
With a lash of its fish-hook tongue.
But there's something about me

And nodding, Ha Ha demurs,
And keeps its weapon out of range.
Perhaps Ha Ha's found
A fault or two in my confidence,
And the further
Into this conversation we go,
My intrigue will grow,
And together we will open up.

'I was sick of heaven's uniformity,
Its blissful purpose,
And the blinding white.
White, white, everywhere white!
The clouds, the linen, the daily mizzle,
Angels' waste is always white,
While mine's a brownish mixture.
And I admit, I became rebellious,
I am the hell father to black humour.
I wonder from where hatred comes,
But come it does, real and mad.'

'Hombre the omnipresent? It lives
Here in my heaving chest.
It questions not, letting things be,
And where else can a redeemer live?
We share common shelters,
Hombre and me,
And as it now happens
This blob off Granville's coast,
A place I'm fond of, a place of mirth.'

Ha Ha sees that I daren't divert my eyes,
In fact, I feel like I've been hypnotised

By its sweet pre-pubescent voice,
Like Mickey Mouse's before his voice broke.
Ha Ha coo's like the ocean's swell.
It has heard me speak similar,
When I was fearful of my dominant dad.
And though I'm afraid,
Ha Ha sees I'm fascinated by its malad charm.

'You are not the first to see yourself
As likely you really are;
Your mind filled with contradictions,
With guilt and self-deceptions.
You can see them in my eyes
Projected by you, from your ego.
You and I are one
As I am with my kind;
There is no original sin.
Rather it's me, a secret gene
That is embryo imbedded.
Our destinies are simultaneous,
As you've experienced
In your primary school days.
The early signs
Of my mischievous presence
Starts with bullying.
Hombre hangs around there for sure,
And we finish the other's work.
I sense your quivering discomfort.
I like that in my serious spawns,
For you have no idea what you're doing.
Hombre knows, maybe not
For when it speaks through clergy priests
Its voices blend with mine,

137

Messing clergy priests up on sins.
And boy do they stumble!
Though you stumbled differently.
Superior are these curly clergy
Standing before their brittle flock,
Safe they are from a judge's gavel,
Matey mates like a ring of Saviles,
Who? Oh, I know!
And then one of them snoops.
Oops!
And he lifts a little girl's frock,
A little lamb hidden in the flock.
No need to go into extra detail,
I'm not one for explicit material.
I like hypocrites, they burn better.
Slow fires work well on oily skins.
I like the way hypocrisy sickens
The general public and diabolos like me.
Brother actors they are, faultless not.
Oh they'll pray and then deny,
And run for parish cover,
Before their stench goes public.
Federations of flies buzz around
These professors of the 'oly 'ible,
(I cannot utter this phrase in toto)
Swarms and swarms pest them,
For they love the hypocrite's dung.
True, not all 'oly men behave this way;
They should though,
For my fires are always hungry.
I am satisfied, there's plenty of return,
In fact, a tasty piece is soon to come.
He died in a state of holy grace,

But got at boys when acting like clergy.
Born out of Roma, a place forbidden,
He'll lie prostrate on an offal slab.
I'll have his innards sent out west,
His gonads posted up north,
Tongue'll go south, his heart east.
And all this grief I'll duly spread
For bishop maladapts
And their Hombre to get to work,
And try and patch things up,
By asking for absolute forgiveness.
Bad clergy who plot revenge,
Ignore my whispers
At their pernicious peril!
Worlds of Good and Evil collide
When men and the Hombre co-depend,
Each more sacred than the other,
When hearts are dipped in power.
Here's the collateral damage,
The broken children's bodies
Gazed upon by their parents,
In my baleful presence.
All the righteous are in a rage,
Their conscience is no marker,
And blood and deceit premixed
Make an appalling soil.
If there's blame, then blame me,
But the price to pay is homage.
I epitomise evil; yet I am no crooner!
I dive into the devilish unconscious;
Associations and slips flow freely
And break into abstract words
And I reassemble them,

For ordinary humans to understand them.
I was simpler in ignorant times.
I was art at its greatest!
Dore's winged demon, a stunner,
Not Eve's betrayer, but Ein Conner,
Magnificently flawed and fragile!
I've no love for psychology,
I prefer believers retell their stories
About my demise as Archangel #1.
How I rose above the sun
To fall then, to the darkest of depths.
Though my illicit soul was confined
In absolute loneliness,
It is by the grace of serendipity
That I remain undead!
And I, unclean, though diminished,
Still find I am quite acceptable to me.
And new experiences beckon me
To go on with my hellova life,
Far removed from mental illness.
My will is free, thanks to gothic belief!
I'm always desirable to the superstitious
As I hover in their minds,
Garrisoned by delicious unknowns,
Sought for and embraced unconditionally.
First in a babe with minor knowledge
Until old age snatches vitality away.
When dead, I leave corpses to their own,
When dead, flesh is of no use to me.
The senses gone, whither temptation?
What is it about character weaknesses
That sustains moral diseases?
Poor aimless souls

Floating around this murky earthen-sphere.
Boy do I have a way with words!
Me, this manitou,
Speaking of my darkness.
And I like flattery too, and this is good.'

Though I am no threat
I'm unsure if I'll leave unscathed,
That's if Ha Ha decides to allow it.

'True, I have inspired
Great artwork and literature,
And discordant manners,
An archangel to them all!
Let the bad scum float the surface
After the final deluge,
And I will be their final judge.
The hypocrites and liars
Will be treated harshest,
And Heaven will expunge them.'

I nod to Itself.
Is there a prize for me?
I've hoped for a new debating friend
Who questions my transient demeanour.

'And you'd be right there, matey!
My domain's the established rust,
And it grows daily.
It's coming around your corners
Looking for the latest malcontents,
Like those you've left behind.
I like non believers,

For when there's mass panic
And anarchy,
I get to enjoy the accusations,
Even atheists put the blame on me!
Bring it on!
Bring on Ha Ha Satan's cursing!
I'm as patient as
My immortal being depends.
I will continue to find
Enquiring minds in search of me.
I'm designed to comfort,
And manage bad habits.
I take them unto myself,
So you dreamers
Can fulfil your death wishes.
All born to die shall know it,
Not universally told, but devilinely.
For love that's rarely divine
Lulls away when troubles brew.
I'm right here to assist,
When despair is overwhelmed
By the bad stuff.
I am no demon:
If you toss me like a coin
Statistically at random,
You'll get the hombre's side as much.
It may surprise you, but I am fair;
I do not need absolutes,
Nor need I preach for targets.
I am satisfied with diversity,
And the pious do not threaten me,
Nor do criminals when they fault.
Clever me who knows

That all who live and die
Are luckily my disciples!
Hombre or Satan, toss a coin,
Worship is as worship does!
I prefer non believers, either way,
Brave bodies doing well,
Unconsciously under my spell,
And I allow flexibility,
For I wish not to stub individuality.
Look at you, Frank proud,
A mirror to me,
And looking ever so casual.
You, the rebel son of Hombre,
Will always doubt yourself.
And hickory, dickory, dock
Frank rewinds his clock.'

Canto Seven

The Demon's chorus:
HA HA SATAN WASN'T SO CRUEL,
THIS LONE DRIFTER, ALL WIND BLOWN,
WON'T BE FORGED INTO HIS TOOL,
NOR BE GORMLESS, NOR BE GA GA.

I've returned to an amiable sea. Its gentle bumps massage my keel.
It was a dream, wasn't it? Me and Ha Ha Satan.
Its boly-woly voice had echoed from a polysyllabic shore,
To a space deep inside my skull.

Strange feelings enter my chest, and weakened, I lie down to rest.
This ocean could defer new disasters,
And save its dross and blasters for I walk as though on casters.
Come tomorrow, gulls and terns will check upon my ungainly gait.
I'll give them piqued answers to their routine questions of my journey,
Since I've prepared them while still angry.
But where is that running pen? Gone with a sea mist, has it done?
I might use moonlight instead and ink my strange story
Over my chestnut body.
My skin, like a cured papyrus, is etched with my struggle's sores.
I'd like to find readers versed in the ways of sea drifters,
Like in Boy's Own and Kipling Tales.
Someone who appreciates the maddest dares,
Done with aplomb, and no cussing,
When the hero slays adversity with instinct,
When knowledge and true grit is armoury for reader joy.

Here then is my real need.
To satisfy with quality, and like the poets,

Lead an idea into its life and truthfully follow it.
I've had this method, when in blind faith
I tossed myself into the mix, at bingo, at church,
Playing backyard cricket.
All in all, chancing my arm and fluking it.
That is how I understand change, without contrivance,
Without calculation, blind luck would do it.

My storm wounds are open cut, criss-crossed over my parchment skin.
In the fine airs of clouds my compound thoughts
Hurry across this deepest sea.
Thoughts from early baby cries, the gaps I've sought in memory.
There is too much missing, and as for my damnable actions,
Ha Ha Satan is forgiving.
For Him is I, and I am Him, says one to the other.

I'm resting in my dinghy, thinking of porridge and toast,
Of a bowl of hot Campbell's soup,
Roast potatoes and vegies, ambushing a chicken roast.
I've relished them and bacon smells, when absolutely hungry.
But I'm too weak to think, except to not be turning back.
Good ideas leave me as soon as they arrive.
Away they go, down back alleyways, down the gutters.
I think of promises made to myself, and to little Granville. Promises.
Today put off, tomorrow browsed, responsibilities left unhoused.

These crafted clouds are a better place for mental stuff to fly to.
They remind me of my latent love for nature,
And where my aspirations should truly go.
Here white landscapes fill 'til grey,
Moistened droplets gather and return to the welcoming sea,
Reconnecting my awe to some osmosis;
Clouds do alter my perceptions.

Sometimes they look like factory gasses.
I sadden when my good intentions are not loud enough.
I feel powerlessness and cannot overcome easy adversities,
And I dismiss expectations.
Always do they run backwards into my misery.

Now my pained memory speaks and I'm coolly walking,
As that homeless Frank dressed in rags,
Mentally ill but looking alright,
A post seminarian living out of bags,
Striding on footpaths at shopping malls,
And though I am alarmingly bright,
I misread graffiti written on brick walls.
Here were hard self-talks, my Granville roots indiscrete,
I struggled with depression, a tough practice, and a double feat,
My failure was my open-cut wealth.
In loneliness anxieties stalked, and lead me blind.
My foolish vanity entered black, for the morrow's disdain,
And my confidence that was smothered.

I'm facing another tepid night, on a sea renowned for its moods,
A change, a Roaring Forties whim, my gaze turns back seeking the coast,
A place close to where I set sail,
A place of death, on the edge of lands.
Tragedy is lost on anger which curtails repair,
Slower when denial intervenes.
Ideas die and no one speaks, death is a language a few seek,
I am confused by fate's clauses, who is to blame, what are the causes?
Time for my discomfort to be documented.
There's no sorrow until powers agree,
And approve progress implemented,
And regret is homely, over a pot of tea.
When history repeats itself right, and truth is honestly written,

The naive and the sensible, bond with the guilt-ridden.

Some questions I shouldn't ask.
Necessity reveals my madness in my downbeat shuffles to emptiness,
In the mundane, in my self-searching,
In my sleeping body slowly dying.
Surrealist thoughts assist my slowing.
A dark night is my tomb.
I've urgent rest, I've my hallucinations.
Come another dusk, having supped on visions that come to pass,
I will again prepare for the morrow as though compromised;
For my tired days feel like weeks.
And though I've mistrusted my roots,
It's comforting to know I was once there.
I can't remember my little playtimes,
Nor the significance of childhood.
I've thought of what might have been, and where I haven't been,
And the type of person I could have been.

In this puny vessel that skates the trifling sea,
The body clock in my sun-hawed body
Has worked no better in this prison cell.
I dwell in twin time viewing and acting on my reactions,
Just like the Ha Ha did, and completely outside itself;
Like an eggshell is to yolk, invulnerable until disposed of.
My spirit is lured to adventure and as a new dawn breaks,
I'll snuff my fears and battle on.

Canto Eight

The Demon's chorus:
LOOK OUT, HE'S MOCKED HIS LUCK,
PUFFED HIS CHEST, BLUFFED THE WIND,
IS IT NOW, HE'LL LOSE HIS PLUCK?
OR FIND THOREAU IN HIS NOOK.

To feel reinvigorated after I awake,
To be possessed by a morning light,
And feel clean, from remembered dreams the night before.
I know my five buoys, my propping senses
Are as sharp as a bodkin, and ready for some work.

Washed and brushed and bread-fed,
I shall navigate this dinghy to rest upon that shore horizon near.
An unsurprising shore that came unto me,
When I simply wished it.
I have become sick and tired of confusing myself.
The sea's bland surface reminds me of play time in the dark.
The shore yonder appears flat enough, and if I miss a beach,
Land will halt me short of obliteration.
I've been a floater too long, and had weightlessness,
And reactive voices: I'd like peace, but not to shrink.
Get out of this can man, get onto a piece of land.
Try another tack, try newer smells,
And crash the dinghy on yonder sand bar.
On arrival I'll write on the sand with my feet,
And be its explorer in a reverent nod to Captain Cook.
And my weight increases as I near this shapeless shore.
I'll name it Ha Ha Satan's Stool, for it sure looks a brown pattie,
Sandy scrub, and boggy moor, the colours of a demon's shame.

This will do, this marshy meadow: time for me to cast a glance,
Walk this small isle and graze romance.
A potent chance is there for me to find an isle's secrets,
Created, so that I might practice what I think.
I wipe my boots and lace them, my legs will be lead actors for the part,
My feelings are swelling up my heart.
The dawn auburn sky is its brightest hue,
The day urges out a hope now due,
For me to stop and make a stand and be the explorer of this land.
Hat is donned, sunglasses lit, I'll go walking until I'm spent,
And be sure to outwalk the sun.

On landing, a cicerone breeze tells me where to plant my feet.
"Walk then," resounds the whirl.
And upstanding I survey the gentle rise,
A fantasy place for me to use my marvellous legs,
That my sea sojourn has ignored.
And the breeze alerts me to the meditations walking does.
"Take a sauntering walk," it riles.
"Go with an honest heart!"
Strong walking avails me to this isle.
I might turn out my senses, and refocus away from restlessness,
And search for a sense of place.
And tho' hardships seem aplenty I walk over creek and tussock,
Striding like an overlander looking for fresh artefacts.
Though I cannot name the plants, and crushed by my ignorance,
I am at one sylph of knowing that this place, abundant with nature
Is not for conquering, but for my respect.
I'm going about with good walking, for pace stimulates precious time,
That I might do some knowing, and stretch my visions further.

The leaving sea motivates me, and the dinghy angles and rests,
And I walk in my Dryzabone, henna red to match my hair.

149

The storm winds have left their mark on this infant landscape,
Scratched by the same elements that plays upon my moods.
I feel an affinity with the island, bleak and rough and lonely,
Though smelling a little off.
I will spend my energy and my sweat will vigorously run.
I can stroll with care, until the sun's lamps dim.

As I walk, I protect masked boobies and sooty terns,
Protecting their nests.
They swan dive, and I bow my head to the birds which use the land.
And now I take the mantle, and begin my strident test
Of conflicting values on this narrow waste land.
"Walk, not dream," says the breeze.
"Feel the joy beneath your feet.
This space is your wilderness."

I begin to name land what I see after the mistakes I have made.
Dismal. Snap-billed, Crawling, Low Head on a Buttress Rising,
Freshwater stilled upon Loner's Cleft, Monotony, a Horizon's Best.
Good names, which keep desperate anonymity close by my side.
I step lightly as I go, size eights on muddy ridges.
Soul footprints to be washed away in the next pulsing rains.
My imprint must leave like a flower's scent through air.
I'm walking beside fanatic traffic losing myself in the cluster,
Loosening my clotted self.
A practiced spectator of the weather,
I'd sit for hours and watch black cormorants amble across the sky,
And sunsets bleeding blood red into clouds and early evenings.
There's an affinity here to when I was walking Granville streets
Thinking I'd got away from it all; walking rather its byways,
And the trails to Stukeley's grotto.
But I am as nervous here as there and I'm like a descending bird,
I am respectful toward the land.

My future's in my parted hands, spread heavenward as I sit
Upon a boulder, taking rest.
I slowly consume water and my snacks, and listen for life around.
Birdsongs, and of gleaming shallows, and quiet around a slender glen.
A venerable sun is lenten too, and shy behind draft horse clouds.

Midday's are my lunchtime hours.
The need reminding me that I'm still the habitual man,
Whose address is Granville, a sea-bird's flight away.
My agendas disrupt the hour, how they squabble, my petty thoughts.
I'm not half the man Stukeley is, say the harrowing breezes.
Yes I nearly am! Frank's lowest portion;
My feet ordained by Stukeley, for them to worship raw surfaces.
I must think of values, and not dismiss or loathe aridity,
For that and air, connect me to my surroundings.
By the by my troubles should phalanx and peter out,
My awry selves reconnecting, thanks to beautiful walking.

Thinking, as I sit and rest, of myself the eager Frank surfing bibles
Back in my cave on Muscle St.
I revered them as though divine, like the docos about Lake Eyre,
Its dry times and its wet.
I am there, when not here, sitting, watching, in a stare,
Walking about in biblical scene, sitting on a dreaming rock,
How languor fools the dreamer!

Henry David Thoreau loved walking Stukeley told me,
A man who spoke when walking with his god,
And to friends who walked beside him.
He wanted poets to express the beauty of the wilderness.
They must do this while they walk, and make their walking poetry.

Another day dawns like a homily. The air's sweet fragrances come early.
I really don't understand the alchemy, and yet I love it even more.
I walk this island and break away from the nightmares.
I wonder what Concord was like, Thoreau's little village.
About which Stukeley had said. A village surrounded by tilled red soils.
And forests, wild and welcoming, for Thoreau to go tramping them.
And when he'd return in the evening,
He'd put his experiences to the page.
Stukeley said he had his critics.
And yet his influence is long impressed upon nature loving minds.
I am walking with a tune, up and down a golden dune,
Like a war soldier due for change, by surviving, or sleeping.
And while engrossed in my reflections,
The sky has turned a darkened spread.
The first stars phosphoresce and I love them too; for I now feel safe.
I'll walk until my raw bones cry out for sympathy.
I'll soon be a swelling mass; for my bones are near stiffed.
And aged in likeness to old growth;
A useful link, and a possible creed for me to keep and follow.
Patience is a paramour to generations not walking.
Heirs to plastic plants rooted in plastic urban pots.
I'd dearly like to remove concrete when I return to Granville.
I'll get the council permits, and I'll tell the soils underneath,
They are for tilling, and for the trees,
For birds to sing in them.

Canto nine

The Demon's chorus:
AS IF A JOKE FALLS WITHOUT A LAUGH,
HIS ORDINARY ROOTS ARE SOON REVIVED,
BLOOD DRAINS TO HIS LOWER HALF,
TO ESCAPE A BRAIN BUZZED BY ITS JAZZ.

Late afternoon blends with eventide.
And after sunset I'm watching nature's time that is for sleep.
The night is cool in late autumn, and in the open air,
I'm enjoying the breeze's seraphic somnambulism,
And then along comes Thoreau himself.
We were introduced back in Granville.
And now we lay together under moonbeams
Sharing the same dream, in thrall of a dark night's beauty.
We're ringed by whispering swamps,
Distant Tufa terraces and mound springs.
Ecosystems like in Thoreau's age, and we lay together, hand in hand.
Our eyes portals for stars to enter;
And our shared outlooks energise our kinship, wonder and enterprise.
The moon's bright halo matures this ancient island,
And naked lands elsewhere.
We two founders of the Fifth Estate:
We familiar ghosts are granted by nature to walk nether lands.
We enjoy each other's company, and the pleasures of walking.
In our dream we walk to a lookout and spy
Each of our townships, like awed foreigners.
Gazing east we see prismatic light, gazing west we see the same light
Daubed over our twinning towns.
Grasses greener, homes are simpler, townscapes muter,
Mountains higher.
Small joys in their new world, the brightest suns in Granville,

And in Concord.

And come the dawn, I'm fed, toileted and relaxed,
Having walked this isle and spied another not too distant,
I set sail to that island yonder.
My dinghy finds a glassy sea, not a breath of wind to act as muscle.
I must paddle with a prop, and though my arms are weak,
My soft hands spread like wings.
And through the water I now glide, paddling like a naughty surfer
Toward a shoreline like no other.
Antipodean swells heave and rise and then quickly disappear.
As I paddle closer an impenetrable rampart begins to rise.
I see the swells retreating on contact, their power thus diminished,
As though the waves sink undersea.
I cannot understand how the wide, rising waves are pacified
When they hit this barrier wall.
I paddle closer, and I'm no more than a yell's faint echo away
From this stark stone wall;
I watch the scene of crashed waves disappearing.
And imagery begins to show like illuminate cave paintings.
The tincture of these carvings reveal familiar images;
Like I've seen in National Geographic. And the paintings come alive.
A thousand screens within a screen which display,
Love, birth, vitality and death.
Weather, landscapes, the universe, desert fauna, cities, tribal folk.
All who've lived or might have been, in chaos in the order of things.
Images brilliant like asteroid flashes, opaque and winnowed by weather.

I paddle to find a breach along this wall metres high,
That surrounds this island three spans wide.
Around again, I cannot reach it. Around again, I begin to read it.
Somewhere here is my story, one image or many that must be mine.
Somewhere here is the junction of my past and present;

154

A hegira to be, in my upward climb.
Paddling around a dozen times I see familiar likenesses.
Perhaps a school photo, and my grave.
Something that says Frank O'Connor.
And I grasp at it, and alight, and begin to climb the sheer wall face,
Clasping at the story grooves, over family and over foes,
Over Catholic representations, over significant others here and there.
I slip on a mother but find my own, and I climb over my present life,
And see myself as priest on a screen inverted and colourless,
Descending the same path I am now climbing.
I soon realise when bodily pain demands oblivion,
That vertigo is not for me.
I touch the wall's sulcus, but not my intimate details.
There's something cloying about them,
Something slippery, something gross.
And I climb toward my future,
Like a fretting Digger up Gallipoli's hill face.
My lungs take one long breath, and I reach the wall's hillock,
And on its summit, I am standing,
Stunned to find I've climbed just metres.
Breathless as though atop Mt. Kosciusko.
I dare not look skyward again.
And casting my eyes downward I see an uninteresting view.
A pancake plain except a yonder hill.
Not a blade of grass or trunk of tree.
And I jump off the wall, and head across a sandy flat.
Just once do I look back at the wall, and I see
A smiling boy with Downs Syndrome sitting atop, waving me goodbye.
As I walk, signs appear this way and that,
TO THE KEEPER OF THE FISHERMAN'S RING.
This way TO, this way TO. TO a curvaceous hill afar.
It LIVES in ALIENATION.
The ONE who keeps the Fisherman's Ring.

As remote as the moon's dark side. Far indeed from heaven!
On nearing the hill, I see how it resembles a breast,
Well formed as lumpy lava allows,
One of nature's glorious perfections.
I am sauntering near, drawn as if a looter moth,
Intrigued by hints of symbolism which hangs on crosses beside the path.
These look like runes from ancient tombs,
Symbols pagan to these agnostic times.
Were they made by heretics who sheltered in dank and gloomy caves?
These crosses shabbily built for mad martyrs.
A mummified body lies exposed, a half-beatific smile,
Holy and against reason.
And then I see decomposed fish nailed through the gills.
'You are not who you think you are.'
A severe voice suddenly says.
I've heard that voice before, and it alters my mood
From the curious to a combatant.

The breast looms larger as I approach.
Its curvaceous shadow takes me as I walk.
And in it I come to a low and grubby glass door, and stop.
I peer into the glass and see a pagan man.
He is clothed in a white suit. His hair is rather long.
I appear to be what I thought I never was.
The door opens to an incense smell. An artificial female voice says,
"Please enter. How are you today?
Is there anything I can help you with?"
No. Thank you, I say. "Have a lovely day, won't you sir."
And above the doorway is the final sign that reads,
ERAWEB DOG.

Canto Ten

The Demon's chorus:
WHILE HIS LOYALTIES ARE UNDERDONE,
HE'LL FIND A PLACE, SOMEWHERE NICE,
MEET A NEW FRIEND, HAVE SOME FUN,
AND EACH WILL SHARE THE OTHER'S BILE.

Caution is the robber's tool, suitable to one far sailed by stealth.
I, a swag known as Frank,
A robber who stumbled first on the leading sandstone slab,
That descends into musty darkness.
And down a stone spiral staircase I tread and pass and speed,
Down through human torments that inspired Dante Alighieri,
Down and down into a gulping earth, deep into the Palaeolithic Age,
Deep into Jules Verne's vision of Gaia's secret core.
I speed and speed, and finally an aureole hits my eyes
Illuminating a dirty grotto.
And sitting there on a Shaker throne is this Keeper in pallium white,
Shapeless like a curtain, a cloak hiding its doubtful gender.
Its eyes twinkle mischievously, its lips are Mona Lisa pursed,
And it has a geisha presence.
The embroidered skullcap upon its head,
Is peaked with fake spinach leaves.
Its left arm is clenched across its chest,
The bare right arm is extended prone,
Twice as long as it's left, and which rests upon a butcher's slab.
A brass ring rounds the third finger of the repose, pallid hand.
Its veins reveal their delicate patterns, like flooded tributaries.
And a cleaver stands beside the slab, the blade blood stained,
And so is the stone-lined gutter extending beneath the bloody slab.
The keeper breaks into a fiendish smile, its controlled placidity
Has disturbed this robber visitor.

I sit before this effigy, and the three stuffed toys fronting it.
Wombat, Mickey and Bumble Bee, satiric metaphors for the Trinity:
The humour of it softens my stare.
And in the dominant silence I am perplexed,
For two odd brothers have just met and will now settle.
Neither of us have any plans it seems.
We are both comfortably alienated.
The question of our futures is long lapsed,
Our time enters détente, and silence is void of place.
We look into the other's eyes, and search for life within our silences,
A life that was, and no doubt yet to come.
There are ways to control time.
Through chronometers and sun dials. By the timing of seasons.
By the birth and death of everyone. By tragedy underpinning hope.
Time and silence that's incremental,
When all that passes, passes into silence.
Silence, the crucial seed that germinates great meetings.
To abuse it, or not? Make argument or discourse?
Make threats or consensus? Our brain waves synchronise.
And from out the silence, a soliloquy begins.
The Keeper's pleading eyes
Are my hints to answer the dilemma of its catatonia,
That appears to plague this creature.
And true, it looks uncomfortable sitting on its namby-pamby throne.
I am underwhelmed, indifferent but I'll stare at the Keeper.
Stare, and keep staring as the soliloquy canters along,
Until I hear its English words, unscrambled and unscrabbled,
Through a telephone earpiece hovering nearby.

'What is to be done with us? Humbled priests named Peter.
The Saviour's bedevilled offspring, most excellent persecutors,
And carousing schoolmen, who imitated holiness best!

We mock our voluptuous image, and are scorned for feeling scorned.
We can only mutually adore. How sexual desire flogs our souls!
Two-thousand-year-old Peters, alchemists of good vs. evil,
And self-appointed regulators over the tyranny of nature:
It wasn't enough to lust for our faithfuls,
Complicit obedience, we had to destroy!
Only in joyous cruelty do we offer salvation:
By imagining goodness in our unconfessed sins.
Because, from churches of fear have shepherd priests come,
And if truly there is no God there will always be the Mimics.
In the face of human suffering if we insist on our relevancy
We must think of ourselves as frauds, the faithful the opposite,
And let Satan be the one to figure out who is really fooling who!'

The squirming Keeper shifts in its protective tepee.
Its discomfort almost topples its inconvenient throne.

'We are the end of a line of street blind vicars,
Squinting from the See, smelling like the old city's halitosis.'

Its short arm points to roughly sewn words on its tunic.
I am the last of the number 2's the words say.
This thing has got into my head the same way Ha Ha did.
And neither will it now leave.

'Listen to my story of past and future illusions;
How the challenges to my authority was strongly dealt with,
By priestly love; with fire and through sword.
The logic of harsh reprisals, and the obliteration of dissent,
Has spread far and wide, even as far as Terra Australis,
When our brethren's delusion were near extinguished,
By the oral narratives of the Indigenous.
And how have we got away with it?'

159

This guilty Keeper is saying it has fled the flames of necromancy,
And abdicated it's so called divine mandates,
To live quietly in Mother Mary's breast.
It is saying it is the last Keeper that will lean
On the impoverished minds of trusting followers,
Fooled by the greatest lie ever told.

'Enough of hypocrisy! Dear Jesus we have lied to you!'

The Keeper twists its anguished face.

'There might well be a heaven; there might well be a hell.
Parallel imaginations make the World.
But there will always be transgressors,
For whom starry eyed God awaits'.

Its withered short arm points upwards.
The fantasy pains of the guilt-ridden Keeper of the Ring
Begins to ache in my head.
This dear leader of the Eucharist is mourning the loss
Of conviction and of live fish, and birthdays thrill no better.

'If there is supreme delight in the discomfort of others,
What say a priestly conscience!
To help the poor, keep 'em poor, rich in number, rich in faith,
So they might know their place, filthy commons in disgrace,
Prayed for by clergy rich in grace, working for their currency.
Never mind the sexually abused, think of abusers facing judgment,
They are men we call brothers, empathy suits not the use of power,
Death will come at any hour, and we'll die in a state of grace.
Do you know how above we are?
We did as we liked to be told, preservation was what was sold,

To understand evil is above and beyond ordinary minds.
It must take superior thinking.
And the disillusioned leave us, and condemn us,
For what, we choose not to understand.
We in the corporation work harder, fighting like all good men
To protect our Catholic airs, even when we condemn the scabs.
You sense cold cynicism, as if our unravelling riddles
Could sit peacefully in heads, or settle in your quiet corner!
If only, if only, if only, if.
The weak and powerless are burdened by the heaviness
Of an unfathomable world,
And they will not ask God to rid them of their God.'

The Keeper's stony face is weeping. I am wondering why the Keeping.
I think I'd better leave, for self pity has a rotten smell.
I am ordinary Frank O'Connor masquerading as a lofty swaggy,
And still my head is throbbing.
The Keeper's alarm and dishabille distracts me.
As a poet, I am naïve.

'Baby please don't go! Stubbornness is an idealist's Achilles heel.
Cynicism its bed of nails'.

These are aching words!
The thumping that's ruining my head is a sick enunciation,
Of the keeper's pathetic words.
I am the bard of Granville, who is yet to pen a lyrical poem.
I am no more than a local fabler inspired by local people,
Indifferent to cosmic forces, except well-placed bets on horses.
Though I am idealistic, I say to myself Granville is where I belong.
The source of my creativity, and the roots of my unmet pain.
It is time for me to go, my cramping legs remind of sea times.
But Wham! Here comes more Keeper paranoia.

'Acute sensitivity is hell for Keepers, and for poets.

There is no escape from pun-packed passion and self pity.
Surely our human spirit is immune from something!
And what of freedom from faith?
There is only natural death, though revolting and absurd.
God, the vicious circle. Circles - the vicious God.
It is a question of balance.
Who will grant unto us the judgement of the great whore?
It is she with whom we kings of the earth have fornicated.
The Holy Spirit, through my dolls here,
Regularly speak to me about these acts,
For if we can make an egg erotic, it would help us.
I swear I've seen the Christ's crowned, bloody face
On my morning toast. See!
I envy disillusioned minds sceptical of Catholic belief,
After the facts of dogma, they are free to have a will.
And yet, in the silence of our guilt we are ever preaching,
Always fraudulent, fulfilling the destiny of a double shame.
You might ask, where did the rolling stone really roll?
And everything priests haven't done the Christ has told us.
Foolishness is bitter brine, when we oddolites try to fake love.
Thou shalt not, thou shalt not!'

The Keeper raises its ten fingers one by one.

'What thou shalt do is better game.
Positive psychology is primed for our destruction.
See! We think like you. Priests are no different to you.
We like honesty and we like truth. We are sick of mental illness.
Enough of black robed mateship. And of grafted blessings.
And is not infallibility but a sheath to forestall disease?

162

Blessed art the Faulty Condom!
In the wake of our failures who should bear this burden?
A real Keeper of course! An ordinary bloke from the 'burbs.
The being of all beings! The brightest of new minds!
The one who has a voice priests fear listening to'.

Canto Eleven

The Demon's Chorus:
FEELING HIS JOURNEY FROM THE START,
HAD SOME PURPOSE, HAD SOME SCOPE;
NOW HIS INHIBITIONS WILL FALL APART,
TO KILL WHAT THWARTS HIS HEALING.

Ah, I've heard all this before;
When Ha Ha ranted in its buoyant mood.
When Stukeley took me aside. I can't do anything about this!
I hate the pain of cruci-fiction; I've seen it in Dali's art.
The Keeper talks of fallibility. And yielding to fraudulence.
Typical of this earthly fraud. Self-promoting. Indamnable.
Ex cathedra, sensus fidelium. The Christ was once a shy boy.
The born-again cynical shine. Is that not you Frank O'Connor?
The Keeper raises its long arm. It has more to say.
The Keeper pleads and insists, and smiles.
And I'm made immobile. My head is in my hands.
The Keeper continues to nag about this great story
Of broken promises, and of good work never done.
Ecumenical priests tell of love and God's hunger,
And of a love stranger than a love for cosmic things.
They who despise themselves when disillusion kicks in,
Are the sick old priests waiting for the big rest.

'We are all actors speaking ludicrous ideals,
And pious fraud like laughing madmen unfastened,
Must have chaotic ends.
What is more primal than the urge to deceive!
And it works!'

164

Its eyes flinch at my knowing smirk.
'Know thyself toward enlightenment!
And shall you have the wherewithal to cleanse my way?
By taking heed thereto according to my own words,
For they are light unto my feet and light unto your path'.

Perhaps Ha Ha is the one really speaking.
It cherishes the disgraced, and it likes a good laugh,
And it loves a mental struggle.
Or nothing speaks to me and the Keeper is phantasy.
Why not grow from guilt? Why not spew bile if it works?
Why not hate for hatred's sake? And feel alive for it.
My legs stiffen. I see a folding chair parked beside the butcher's table.
I sit on it and contemplate this strange encounter.
I am being asked to do something. I am being chosen.
It might be heroic.
The Keeper looks quite infant, like a cancer sufferer nearing death.
The harder I stare at it, the more the sweat rolls,
And spoils the Keeper's painted lips.
Its eyes are a foggy glaze, its skin a parchment grey,
And the tepee tunic disguising its sex crumples in the gloomy light.
The arm upon the table is unmoved.
But the other suddenly grasps the cleaver and swings it in the air,
Slashing through the air.
It swings again, and slashes again.
The Keeper is hinting hard, and laughter, like Ha Ha's rasp,
Accompanies the poetic movement. Cut, cut, cut.
I idly begin to count the swings of the cleaver, as it's maniacally swung.
10, 30, eighty times, above the hand bearing the Fisherman's Ring.
150, 239, and increasing. Then suddenly it stops and hovers.
Bewildered I have slumped into my easy folding chair.

'Would swaggy like to perform this act?
And chop the Keeper's hand at the wrist.
Remove this ring which binds all the Keeper's rings.
Just a few chops at the wrist. It will do us both a world of good.'

The Keeper tempts like Satan.
And the memes of old hurts make their presence felt.
For opportunities like this don't come by very often.
And the promise of another abnormal life beckons.
And while watching the Keeper's cleaver work, I saw a vision.
I saw myself, bloody cleaver in hand riding across barren lands,
Ahead of a ghostly army of tormented victims of inquisitions.
Their last agonies before the flames consumed them are masks,
Which match their blackened skulls.
We reached an isolated castle fortified by fire-breathing stone.
Its ramparts spiked with iron crosses, and Gargoyles protected it.
Our army lays siege for days, and for weeks and months,
Until a final capitulation.
Captives were brought forth and I used a similar cleaver
To sever the head of the castle's lord.
I triumphantly displayed the head which bore
A tattooed number on its forehead.
And though it took just one blow that number is in my head,
The clue also in the Keeper's eyes.
After all, this dream is far from over.
I wonder if all my anger and my frustrated, scruffy body
Could sponsor the blows required,
For I must cut the wrist more than just the obvious once.
What is latent in my mind? What will change if I do it?
Will I leave this place the same? The Keeper suspends its being.
Here's a chance to right some wrongs.
I can take revenge on my parish priest.

166

My demons are still singing, and my only mate never liked me.

'Go on, go on. Do it, do it. Ha Ha Ha, Ha Ha Ha.
You have really come again. Upon your first death,
The mad expectation you'd rise again and redeem a faulty world,
Was left for weak Keepers to explain!
I confess, I confess, me and my company of padre priests,
Aren't up to it. Ha Ha Ha. Go on, go on.
A weak leader knows how and when to lie,
A great leader knows why it is best to tell the truth.
Do it, do it. How long can the good really wait?
Here's a chance for your will to power.
So take up this needy mantle.
Keepers cannot bless for they are cursed,
Ha Ha says so, and so be it'.

I'm off my chair. It thinks I'm Frank-Christ. My head is soundly aching.
I can't stand this anymore and I steady the long arm on the block,
And draw the cleaver from the Keeper.
The calf handle fits nicely, and it smells of rich antiquity.
And I begin the angry chopping.
In my mania I gasp, as each time the hand is severed,
It finds the wrist again. I throw it away; it's back again.
I cut it off and cut it to pieces, and there it is, back again.
There it is, boiled in a pot, there it is, sliced and diced,
There it is, a tongue of fire dancing in the Keeper's grotto,
There it is the jewel in a Big Mac.
This is supernatural madness! There it is, ring and all!
Buried like a dog's bone; there it is, back on the wrist,
Through to the Keeper, playing dead, only kidding!
The violent cutting when I gracefully swing
From air to wrist, is my profoundest poetry yet.

I Frank O'Connor the Delirious, return to my church cricket days,
When I bowled and bowled, not stopping until I got a wicket.
The chopping continues on and on, into the night and the morrow,
A sharpening flint I would borrow.
Strange how the blood is freshly coagulated on the cleaver's edge.
I've gone mad and have lost my sleep.
In glances at the impassive Keeper I perceive its passive face,
Inspiring my demented rage. How dare the Keeper be this forgiving!
The hand's severing must soon end. In death, there is only sorrow.
I defy the Keeper's smirk. The cleaver's blade is blunter.
The severing is getting rougher. 133 and still counting.
The pressure on me is mounting.
My poetic cutting soon becomes doggerel.
Plain and unimaginative. The job must be completed.
I and Ha Ha will feel cheated. A chance like this can't go begging.
I'm no heretic; I'm no saviour. And the blinded shall see.
The Saints are my footy team. I will love them even more.
What I'm doing is truly ghastly. I need not have an audience.
There's no room for a philosophy whereby its ignorance kills.

Sunday and a moonlit night, and I'm on a tea break.
I wished I'd kept my Weetbix bars, water is out of the question.
I battle on exhausted, geed on by Helpmann's choreography.
My number is the lucky one, when I will reach it.
Lately the hand has behaved itself, after dropping to the ground.
It meekly reattaches itself. None of its flying around.
No flip-flopping headless chicken dances.
Soon it will be all over.
Me and the cleaver become good friends, like a tradesman and his tools.
Cutting the Keeper's wrist is art, though a heavy art,
Formed in narrative poetry.
I mutter a private prayer, for my actions are as needy
As the Keeper sitting here.

168

Affirmation is required, the effort is trebled and thus inspired.
The Keeper's face suddenly lightens. So help me Woo, get this done!
By all the power invested in me self proclaimed, though it be.
And lo! The deed is done. The hand lies flat and dead at last.
The ring has slid from the finger, and I Frank have it in my hand.
The Keeper's patient face broadens into a grateful smile.
It turns away from me and reaches behind its throne,
Bringing out a fishing rod and netting. And up the steps it walks,
Bowing as it passes by me, slumped and tired.
At the top of the passage the beaming Keeper gives me a handless wave.
The bastard. And disappears into the day.
Away from me, pale and gutted.

Canto Twelve

The Demon's chorus:
LIKE A DEPRESSED MOTHER AFTER BIRTH,
WHAT TO DO WITH A SCREAMING CHILD,
AS FRANK O'CONNOR HE UPS HIS WORTH,
AND PULLS THE PLUG FROM A TIRED DYKE.

Who sits upon this vacated throne? Frank O'Connor or the New Keeper?
In the winter of nineteen seventy-four. Time is needed to catch a breath.
All that severing, and no death. All that energy for more despair.
The handless Keeper wanders free. And what of the Holy Hot Seat?
Shall it buckle at its legs? I might have gone too far.
Thinking of Che and revolution. Thinking of world wars and renewal.
This ring has a saccharin power and maybe I'll walk away.
Leave the ring to the dust. These thoughts are for today.
As for tomorrow they won't say.

I'm a fence for roaming sheep, a ghost author of the Good News,
And a parody of Ha Ha itself.
Every idea is possible to me on this gotcha throne.
I'm ragged and bearded, and I might forget Granville,
And take up hermit living, like my mentor Stukeley.
I'm looking like a shabby priest, though my tired eyes radiate warmth,
For my crimson soul is burning. Am I not now a drag-net for seekers?
The natural whose insights grew from heresy,
Whose will was always going to be free.
A glorious mystical vision begins to grow,
Working hard against my cynicism.
How should I prepare to run a new world order?
This may well be my calling, imagining a new wellbeing.
Find joy and joy, and more joy and spread it all around.
My ignorance is self revealed, life really does begin after death,

170

My short Catholic life having died.
And might I be a reaper in-waiting for expectant lost souls,
Who yearn for an authentic faith?
Souls who find little comfort in the triple speak of liturgy.
Would Stukeley approve? I say to myself, or is it he?
Great Frank, you are the blackest night; play not semantic games.
Inspired Frank, fill hope with Iona's light;
And kill every impostor.
Sharp Frank has got Ha Ha's measure;
They who do, do out of self will.
Humble Frank; learn to be deeply loved;
Give ladder rungs no space.
Fragile Frank if you are to be dismissed;
Leave with your grace intact.
Earnest Frank, dissolve your insecurities;
And trust only yourself.
Radical Frank, if you go to new extremes;
Remember your basic needs.
Dreaming Frank, if your ideals are reckless;
Keep sober the eve of death.
Unknown Frank, the world owes you little;
But still it may suggest,
'You are not who you think you are.'

I've often wondered why Holden driving Ruffians
Smash rival Fords parked on concrete Aussie flags.
Their empty tinnies and their sedans,
Strewn about the public sands, hooning over public lands:
Is it their respect for the colonial aftermath?
And why do Catholics love rosary and roast beef dinners,
Fags and alcoholic fumes, arguments over wrestling mania,
Slagging believers beyond their fringe, cracker nights and the housie?
And mad auntie's horribly bad breath?

171

Though I gag I must endure it.
Why do cheeky priests stick their crosses on shoe soles?
On white hankies and blue undies, and if they want to, up their arses.
Hide embarrassment like a lurker, foul language is aimed to jerk ya!
I've never thought about it.
Why is pub noise quieter than a lonely drinker's silence?
That when all's well that ends well the people are nice and good.
I know how a poet's manuscript finishes up in a shredder's pile,
For it talks of ending uncertainty by collapsing its form,
And finding certainty in something else.

And when Granville Ruffian body temperatures seed
The energy of their malevolence, they are displaced into burning blue.
And violence was a light for them to use sarcasm against me,
Full of it.
Winds and fires keen my haste, exciting my need to be chaste.
I, Frank pinch myself. How lucky to live in Granville times!
I've heard a country pasture's quiet jump over the city's wide edge.
It is a landscape aware of itself. 'It is what it knows it is.'
When the sun ripens Granville at the end of a peaceful day,
There are reasons to be hopeful.
Residents prepare for future sunsets, the spectrum of the reds they bring.
How does an ordinary bloke rule? By reflecting on the day's sunset.
I'm exhausted and cannot move, and I fall asleep again.

The ring is in my grasp, and though sleep will relax me
My left hand will keep a Goliath grip,
The ring mustn't slip, nor be sacrificed to Gollum's greed,
Nor be lost in this dingy grotto, hidden under this island's breast,
Not so far from Granville.
An unremarkable ring that searched for insignificant me.

I awaken and still I am tired, and sit depressed,

Upon my long-hat throne, worrying in lateral ways,
And the logic of the ring's power says my fate is certain.
As wishful thinking had inbred with Catholic fantasy,
Fraud is therefore refurbished with fraud.
As my space surrounds another,
My melancholy begets insecurity,
From melancholy can come fear,
From fear dissonance, and in dissonance aggression.
My reactions rebound in my emptiness,
Away from my heart and back toward my wishful thinking.
My chaotic wilderness though average, is too busy,
To examine self-esteem and bring it before the light.
In violence I've been remade, though I've found confusion.
The more I've changed the more I'm changing.
Old dissent was conceived in Catholic sorceries,
When nude Popes bathed and dried the Virgin Mother's sex,
And still her flowing menstrual blood did not free them!
My Granville biography is affecting; my poetry has inspired violence.
I'd been a sponge for fantasy, and what I've learnt mystifies!
Magisterium or the Christ bursts!
The Keeper had desired to cure belief and hungry cynicism.
But what have I really ended?
A dream? A fantasy? A wish hoped for?
Am I still a swaggie head, or a baby lyrical poet?
Also known as Frank O'Connor, who is not what I think I am.
An ordinary bloke with a funny name, and the misfit fits.
But with a mentor like Stukeley and with a guardian angel like Woo,
There must be something else I should do.

Part 4

How Frank became the Horned Bouncer

Canon 22 – Frank's Wit will shine through the Harsh Cadence of many rugged Lines

The Demon's chorus:
FRANK HOPPED A BARGE BACK TO SHORE,
WHAT TO DO ABOUT HIS SHAKING HAND,
HE SPENT A LONG TIME THINKING SOME MORE,
STUKELEY AND HIS SISTER HE WOULD THANK.

Frank had awoken to a new day, still a drifter as he was before his epic journey, travel weary, and he made himself ready to walk again. He was living like a beggar, depressed, wandering within reach of his former childhood home, where his older sister secretly fed and supported him. Then suddenly one day, as if Stukeley spoke to him, he found the strength to leave suburbia for the wilderness of the Blue Mountains west of Granville, to find solace in nature, imagine it, and forget his past. It was not only the thoughts of Stukeley which inspired him, but also it was his sister's wish that he should do so, for she could no longer support him.

Over time Frank became self-sufficient, having learnt bush-craft from Stukeley, it was here in the bush that he began to actuate his conscious presence in nature and nature's presence in him. He began to learn ways of knowing and loving nature through a high state of awareness in which nature became like a mentor, giving him energy to act upon his integrity and values grown from within through his experiences. His demons had set him on the path to atheism yet his spirituality was never in doubt. His cleansing state of mind is who he thinks he is.

Frank began the task of focussing upon his discipline, particularly in terms of his mental health, through his body. He learnt to emphasize meditation in certain circumstances, in certain postures, standing or kneeling, when his self-doubt intervened with his being. There were disciplines of fasting and time-giving, works of compassion, both spiritual and corporeal, and in the caring for animals and birds.

He became primarily focused on efforts to put to death the god distortions which worked his once infant mind. So it was that his external behaviour, habits, attitudes, compulsions, egoist passions, which oppose themselves to the falsehood of a god had him living with nature not only exteriorly, but also interiorly. Frank's purification involved his awareness of his imperfections and finiteness, fostering self-discipline and wisdom. Because of its physical, disciplinary aspect, Frank became as it were a spiritual athlete. Frank sought an understanding of himself in relation to others and to nature, referring not only to his finite fate, but also to maintaining his spiritual, psychological, and physical health.

The activity of Frank's self-reflection enlightened his mind, providing insights into personal truths not only made explicit in his memory, but also those implicit in nature, in an illumination of the depth of his perceived reality and natural happenings, as in the working of the climate, the seasons, the life patterns of humanity, of flora and fauna, making him a whole and thorough being - an acute consciousness of a transcendent order and a vision of life as Frank was making it.

He was learning a higher contemplation, whereby Frank experienced himself as though united with nature. The experience of his union was associated with his love for it, the underlying theme being that nature as his teacher, is known or experienced through his feelings and grown by his intellect, since it is all that is life, and Frank, who abides in this life abides in nature and nature in him. He has no time to be bored and frustrated. He is in no mood to question it.

To see in Frank as the loving friend of nature's creatures, the joyous singer of nature, a keen insight into the innermost world of nature transforming him, was a joy to his imaginary angel Woo. And so closely has the unknown universe and the natural blended in Frank, it is to see in his very asceticism a kind of a system of natural romance. For Frank's singularly vivid imagination is influenced with the imagery of the songs of the winds, and he delights in suiting his action to his thought. So too, Frank's native turn for the picturesque has him uniting with the scenery. He finds in all emerged things, however trivial, reflections of some natural perfection, and he loves to admire in them their beauty, power, and wisdom.

Frank's complex personality fastened on the idea that all from nature are kin by the varying degrees of separation. Hence his custom of claiming brotherhood with all manner of animate and inanimate objects. The personification, therefore, of the elements demonstrate that Frank's growing love of creatures is not simply the offspring of a soft or sentimental disposition. Rather it arises from a deep and abiding sense of the presence of nature, which underpins what he now does. And when he is making a goon-show of music, by playing together a couple of sticks on fallen tree stumps, it is he giving vent to his anger toward cruelty, heart-sore that he is with foreboding at the daunting task of how to challenge it.

Frank's lightsomeness has its source in that entire surrender of everything present and passing, in which his interior liberty founded as a child, is all around him in nature; he drawing his strength from his intimate unions with his surrounds. The mysteries of it, being an extension of the Universe, holds a preponderant place in the new life of Frank, and he has nothing more at heart than to be concerned with preserving nature and learning how to live with it, respectfully and in awe. But he is no Thoreau and it is the thoughts of Stukeley which regularly surface indream.

Stukeley would say that people have a duty to protect and enjoy nature as both the stewards of nature's creation and as its creatures themselves.

178

People should not behave like dissident predators where nature is concerned, but to assume responsibility for it, taking all care so that everything stays healthy and integrated, so as to offer a welcoming and friendly environment. Although these words have not yet followed Frank concerning the bull ant, which have bitten him many a time, causing him to retaliate with anger.

It is a beautiful thing to live within living nature, and by intuiting its behaviour the person over time intuits their own. Frank's growing understanding and experience of nature underscores his whole approach to life and his natural theology. To him all creatures under the skies, each according to its characteristics, unconditionally serve nature. They can naturally love their bodies as themselves by living according to their need to produce and flourish. And humans in community especially, living without the imagined God can get on with their lives as they see fit. They may try to make their lives as vivid and memorable as possible before it comes to its natural end. They are selfish in relation to others, and they reflect upon their actions and are willing to pass on their knowledge. And what truth they find is truth ever consistent with itself, that is better seen than heard. And they need to be on guard that they do not turn away their minds and hearts from nature under the guise of hope and security, separating themselves from their biological connections with Her.

Canon 23 - When Frank finds a place in the Shade of the Underground

The Demon's chorus:
DISCOVERING NATURE FOR WHAT IT MIGHT DO,
CARRIED AROUND LIKE A GOD IN THE HEAD,
THERE WAS THOREAU WHOM HE ONCE KNEW,
HIS ESTEEM FRANK WENT ABOUT RECOVERING.

After Frank's Catholic fall and naturalist re-birth, and having acclimatised his body and mind with the bush, he became a resilient free man and he made himself spiritually ready in order to take the longer-than-Granville plenary walks he now felt he needed to do. His beggardly walks back then were a necessity drawn from his need to stay alive, but now, for his prolonged health and spirits, a saunter with Thoreau through the breadth of a nearby forest, down animal tracks and undergrowth-ways, became mind-bearing. And he should walk like a camel, and think when walking; his inner environment to be drawn from the outside and made into words for him to sing.

The seasons days and nights settle me,

I am born for the starlight and the sun,

The boundaries of the earth remind me,

That I am made for everything within it.

He desired not to be so sedentary, otherwise rusty bones would set in. As he lives more in an upright and mobile manner, the skills needed for sitting still and for watching television, will eventually disappear. He will grow vertical in his habits as the evening of his life approaches. Living much out of doors, in the sun and wind, has so far produced a certain roughness of character in Frank, causing a thicker cuticle to grow over some of the vulnerable qualities of his personality. There has been much more air and sunshine in his thoughts. His callous palms are
180

conversant with the finer moral ingredients of self-respect and heroism, whose touch thrills his heart, rather than the languid fingers of laziness.

His living vicinity in the bush can afford him many a good long walk. And though he has walked almost every day, he has not yet exhausted his reach. A new prospect is a great happiness. A lean-to at the edge of a field not seen before is as exciting as seeing a pyramid. A harmony between the landscape's layout within his walking parameter and the limits of an afternoon walk, has developed in him in the years here on the Blue Mountains an existential relationship with his surrounds.

Frank walks any number of kilometres, without going by any house, without crossing a road except where the possum and wallaby do: first along by a nearby creek, and then a river, and then a meadow and the wood-side. There are square kilometres in his vicinity which have no inhabitant. From many a hill he can see civilization and the abodes of humans afar. The farmers and their works are scarcely more obvious than wombats and their burrows. Not much else occupies the landscape. In a half an hour he can walk off to some portion of the Blue Mountains surface where another human may not have stood for nigh on a year.

His nearest town is the place to which roads come, an expansion of the nearest highway, but is far enough away for him to walk on paths of dirt. He has not so far travelled bitumen as much because he is in no hurry to get to an op shop or the grocers or post office as the town's inhabitants like to do. He carries with him a knapsack which he fills with his needs. And when walking the bitumen for something he needs, there are the polite greetings and nods, and the talk is short. He walks to his sheltered humpy knowing he is talked about, and if he heard them, he chooses to not recognize the words.

In his vicinity, the best part of the land is not private property; the landscape is not owned, and he enjoys comparative freedom. But he knows the day will come when it will be sold to private developers when houses will multiply, and roads will come filled with family cars and commuters. The railway line into the city is a mere twenty kilometres to the north.

There is a subtle magnetism in his bush surrounds, which, when Frank unconsciously yields to it, takes him in the truthful direction. It is not indifferent to the way he walks. His walks take him on the paths he loves to travel, in his interior and ideal world. He often settles in an eastward direction, toward a particular bush area which then takes him out into open fields and winding back roads. The future seems to lie that way to him, and the landscape seems richer on that side. His walking direction is like the outline of a maze, opening and closing eastward, and looking back to where his humpy looks out toward a lowering sun.

After Frank had reinvigorated himself, it was easier for him to step outside and go to a dark corner of the nearby forest, and enter it as though a sacred place. There, for him, is the strength, the marrow, of his being. The wild gum trees stretch over the virgin undergrowth, the same soil which is good for humans and for trees. Here he loses his memory of the frayed edges of civilisation as he encounters it. They fade irrevocably out of his mind. It is only after a long and serious effort to recollect these thoughts that he becomes again aware of his co-dependency with civilisation.

For Frank the weapons with which people ought to use to gain victories, and which should be handed down as heirlooms, are not weaponry and spite, but the pitch-fork, the turf-cutter, the spade, and the back hoe, all moistened with the juices of many a crop, and begrimed with the dust of many a hard-worked field. Dullness is but another name for tameness. It is the non-conforming free whose ways are from wild thinking, who have delighted in sciences and mythologies, whose education hasn't come from formal learning. The wild bird is swifter and more beautiful than the tame. Frank's presence is a light which makes his passion

182

visible, like a lightning flash, and which makes normal light pale in the everyday.

Around Frank is this vast, savage, enveloping mother of his, Nature, cruising like the wind, with such beauty, and companionship for all her children, such as he. That he was so early weaned off nature's breast and given to Catholic society, to that culture which is exclusively an action of a supernatural spirit on humans, a sort of breeding in which produces a certain Catholic nobility, was an attitude destined to limit his individual capacity to grow in the free range.

There is something servile in the need to love laws because they must be obeyed. Laws that are made known to the individual bind societies because they are unreachable. Frank is a child of the mist, who respects the understanding that all are children of the mist. His active duty to himself is knowledge which comes not from legal bondage, but rather liberation from it. All other duty is good only until weariness sets in; and all outsider knowledge is left for the expressions of the artist.

Frank's desire for factual knowledge is intermittent, but his desire to bathe his head in atmospheres mysterious to others is continuous, for him to find empathy in nature, particularly when the morning sun illuminates a spreading mist. But he cannot afford to live without the present. He is blessed that no moment of his passing life is remembered as merely something of the past. Unless he hears the morning kookaburra within his horizon, that memory is belated for the day. Presence is his gospel according to the moment. He has not fallen astern; he has got up early and kept up early, and to be where he is, is to be in season, in the front and centre of time. It is an expression of the health and soundness of nature, a brag for his world, healthiness as of a spring burst forth, a new fountain of the Passions, to celebrate this last instant of time. Where he lives no fugitive laws are passed to control him. Wherever he now goes the essence of nature will go with him. And even if he were somewhere which overwhelms with concrete and glass, he need only glance-look at the sky and he is there.

Frank has been and still is a border lifer. One a Catholic loner he is now a bush loner living on the boundaries of a modern world into which he makes the occasional and transient forays. Nature is a personality so vast and universal Frank fears that he has not fully yet experienced at least one of her features. While almost all people feel a strong attraction for action, entertainment, business, which draws them to society, Frank is strongly attracted to the outside. For the rest how little is the appreciation of the beauty of the landscape which sits obstinately around them! And yet Frank cannot judge others who have made their choices. He asks himself how much of being a loner is loneliness. He has been lonely all his life. And even here in his beloved bush he is lonely still.

Canon 24 - For Frank what Denies will answer Desire

The Demon's chorus:
THORNS AND STICKS POKED AT FRANK'S LIFE,
A METAMORPHOSIS IS NATURE'S RE-BIRTHING,
THERE WAS MYSTERY BEFORE IT WAS STRIFE,
AND FRANK WAS NURSING SORE HORNS.

And then, upon waking, after a peculiar night of turbulence and nightmares, Frank, greatly disturbed by these occurrences, for he had been recently sleeping peacefully without dreaming, found himself to be transformed into a ghastly insect. Alarmed he suddenly stood up on his hind legs and saw other legs, a large lower body, a flat hard stomach, and his head felt as though it moved like a crane. He dare not look any further, and he was suspended in shock, but just as he was about to go into an uncontrollable seizure other ant like creatures came toward him beckoning him with their feelers to come hither, and instinctively he began to do his job.

He was working among a multitude of ants, working and foraging in a great forest. Some ants had remarkably conspicuously elongated, linear trap jaws which could close with a convulsive snap. These jaws appeared predatory to Frank but they actually were the ant's defence. The pincers of these trap-jawed ants were held parallel when closed, but when opened, they opened very wide.

Frank saw these ants had possessed one or two pairs of prominent, long sensory hairs which pointed forward when their pincers were held fully open. The trigger hairs released closure of the pincers, accompanied by a very loud click. And Frank soon realised that he was one of these ants, with large pincers and with a great long hair hanging between them.

185

And that he was a bull ant because of his massive pincer jaws, it meant that he was also employed to stand at the ant colony's nest opening with his pincers cocked. Any alien ant that intruded will have to be struck by Frank; his pincer teeth pinching the intruder's outsides with sufficient force so that he can propel the intruder backwards, preferably through the air, and for some millimetres. In this manner Frank's defence was effectively ejecting alien ants and reducing his own physical risks. Frank was fit enough to spend long shifts at his colony's nest ejecting intruder ant after another, as well as other threatening insects. That he knew which ant to let pass and which to eject was based entirely on his eye for detail; and if that failed then his sense of smell came into play.

Only the queen of the colony had a name, Mary; the rest, the workers, were to Frank anonymous.

Mary's ant colony was shallow and diffuse, consisting of several small chambers among which the adult ants and her brood were scattered. To confuse unwanted ants Mary's chamber was without an obvious entrance. Her nest had multiple narrow, debris-filled entrances from which only one ant could emerge at a time. Solitary workers such as Frank foraged on the nearby ground outside of the nest always with his pincers cocked in open position. Frank also worked alongside other ants whose limbs appeared to have been hacked off. Other workers ants spread diluted honey baits, though no trails were observed; the return of a successful forager apparently stimulated others to emerge from the nest and search nearby in an undirected manner.

Sometimes Frank, rushing about with open pincers, would touch a large object such as a stone and he would snap the pincers against it, and like in a slapstick comedy routine he would fly backwards for a distance of several centimetres, rolling and tumbling as he went. But on landing on proper footing he rushed straight back to the area he was working, and rather than fleeing, in a comedic way he would strike at the same object again.

There came an invasion of fire ants and when the first one entered an opening, the pincer guard struck at it and propelled it backward. After one to three fire ants had been ejected in this manner, and others had gone into unguarded entrances, most of the workers in the nest, including Frank, excitedly emerged and began snapping at the fire ants, dismembering some and shooing others away. These alien ants were frequently flung, along with being injured. The ant's leg or antennae might be broken, and the head capsules of minors were often crushed.

Colony ants like Frank, facing outward with pincers cocked and antennae extended, are like Roman guards assuming the guarding posture. and after remaining motionless in this position for a time, and when there was no threat, they then either backed slowly into the nest, while keeping their pincers open, or are pushed out from behind by the next guard. On occasion a worker guard emerges spontaneously and moved out into the arena. Guards usually crouch to allow nest mates to climb over them, though sometimes they prevented others from entering or exiting, roles Frank seemingly spontaneously performed. Queen Mary never came to nest entrance.

It appeared to Frank that he lived and worked as an ant for months. Though they looked the same Frank found over time, judging by different scents, that he saw new ants joining him at the 'door' of the ant colony, replacing others, many of whom he never saw again. And then one day while he was performing his usual duty of tossing alien ants and other unwanted insects, in one act of throwing he lost a pincer. It didn't hurt but other ants came to him. They began to drag him away but he wouldn't go. And with his remaining pincer he began tossing these aggressors out of the way. They persisted but Frank fought on until eventually they left him alone. And for a time he continued his work, until one day he lost his other pincer.

But rather wait and be torn apart by other ants who saw him as no longer useful Frank went into the forest, found some decaying leaves laying upon twigs and other undergrowth and he crawled in and awaited his inevitable passing into the biological reaches of nature and with Woo beside him.

Canon 25 - And there Hatches Plenty for Frank's ensuing Spring

The Demon's chorus:
THE URGE TO BOUNCE CAME SLOWLY AT FIRST,
A STRANGER SHOWED HIM THE BEAUTIFUL WAY,
A ROLE IN WHICH FRANK COULD BE IMMERSED,
A MAN OF THE CROSS WILL SET HIM FREE.

It was no dream, and after weeks of painful metamorphosis Frank gradually returned to his human self, though, protruding from out Frank's thick red hair above his forehead were now a pair of small horns, like those of a baby goat's, the stubs of ant feelers. These horns were no surprise to Frank. After all, transforming from a human to an ant and back to a human again was bound to have some side effects.

Frank did not yet twig to the clue of his time as an ant. He knew the time had come for a change but he could not imagine how this would occur. He was after all a tramp living in the bush, living off the land, and because he was considered eccentric was treated kindly but a little patronisingly by the village people nearby.

Whenever he went into the closest township Frank wore a slouch hat, a vest over a shirt, dungarees and boots. These he acquired through the local op shop. He wore no underwear and only one pair of socks, all of which he regularly washed in the nearby creek. Though he might look eccentric to others, Frank felt he kept his dignity by dressing well. In human society one's dignity seems incomplete unless there is the approval of others, no matter how rich or poor the person is.

Frank knew no-one by name but he did by sight, always nodding to them as they passed. A very large man, whom Frank had never seen, but to whom Frank nodded, confronted Frank as he passed, telling him to mind his own business. Taken aback Frank simply stared at the man, until the man became aggressive and began to manhandle him. Instinctively Frank grabbed the man, lifted him up and tossed him along the footpath, and for quite a distance. Others came running but Frank, having grabbed his hat lost in the scuffle, quickly left the scene.

Sometime after Frank came across the same man in the town and he warily watched the man pass by. Suddenly the man turned and asked Frank if he had the chance again, in which direction would he throw him. Frank asked the man where he lived. And the man replied pointing in that direction. Frank then replied that that is the direction he would throw him. The man laughed, introduced himself, and told Frank that he was a retired doorman, and if Frank was looking for work, then door man work is the perfect job for him. Frank said nothing and he went back to his humpy.

Again, Frank came across the burly man and again they spoke. The burly man asked if he and Frank could meet somewhere, say the pub, and then he would tell Frank about the job. The man told Frank that, because of his strength, his passive demeanour, his horns, he would never be out of a job, even when he is old. Frank asked why, and the man replied simply that Frank was venerable.

They agreed to meet. Frank was initially nervous for he felt unsure how he would fit back in to society. But then he remembered he was once an ant and ants cannot work together unless they conform to the rules for the preservation of the ant colony. Humans, though somewhat erratic and unpredictable, nevertheless find ways to conform as a society creating a degree of seeming order, if only for the preservation of the species.

Thus, on a Sunday lunch time the burly man Sid, whose nick name was Aunty Jack, and Frank, met in the pub over a steak and a beer and Sid told Frank about his work as a doorman.

Sid told Frank that the best doormen don't necessarily exert violence to solve problems that happen at the door of venues, rather they talk and reason, but if needed they would do the bouncing required. He himself didn't have any qualifications to get regular jobs and so he looked for physical work, and through word of mouth he got a job as a doorman. He knew he could intimidate, and he was impartial to whomever he spoke. His job was to check IDs, keep the peace when lines were long, and deal with unruly behaviour. It's not a pretty job, and because few are willing to do it, there's a fair bit of freedom. And a sense of humour is also required.

Sid said he liked the work. He was useful. He got on well with the bosses. He did get injured. One time he was laid off for weeks after some idiot with a flare gun shot at him and got him in the shoulder. It's being able to work in potentially violent situations without getting violent which is the key. Sid had some martial arts background and the self discipline helped him. The job is honourable. And there was prestige to be had. He had many mates in the game all with stories to tell, and the job wasn't boring. People used to try something on him all the time. He'd just laugh it off, thinking, next.

And you'd learn to pick them. The tossers, the sleaze, the groupies, the top hats. You'd learn who was likely to cause trouble and who weren't. Alcohol was always an issue. Some were happy drunks, but others, males and females, can get real abusive when you don't let them in. A bit of verbal, some shove, and the implied 'toss' did the job. It's all about crowd control. One person can control a crowd provided the crowd knows it needs to be controlled. And for the good of everyone in it. They just want to get inside and have a good time. They know there are rules they have to follow. They'd see him and there'd be respect. He wanted want them to have a good time too. He's got kids, a wife, a mortgage. Everybody wants to go home happy.

You have to dress for the occasion. Being a doorman for a swank club meant you had to dress well. Made the punters feel like they were entering somewhere special. Even strip clubs can be made special. You had to have a good suit, and a spare one in the background, in case someone spewed on you. People think you're there just to do some bouncing. Get in there like a brawler and chuck people here and there so you can show them who's in control. But you're there to keep an eye on things. That's what you're paid for.

Sid told Frank that he knew he could bounce because he's venerable. He can hold things together. The punters 'll know he can bounce them just by looking at him. Frank is taut, fierce looking, and those horns! Yet his eyes tell a different story. He's been hurt. There's been some sort of abuse. He struggles. Sid knows because Sid was abused. But Frank's demeanour says that he won't let that get in the way of doing a good job.

Having to eject a punter from a nightclub doesn't always mean that you didn't manage the job on him or her earlier in the evening. There are the punters looking for trouble, or they can't handle the booze, or their high on something, or they don't get on with people so they make trouble. They'll bring their anger with them and no one knows about it until violence erupts.

Sid tells Frank that no one likes to be asked or told to leave an establishment, especially if they paid a cover charge to get in. If Sid had reminded the guest several times about their conduct then it will come as no surprise when finally, he'd ask them to leave. If he takes the patron aside and discreetly tell him or her about the decision, he's usually reduced the likelihood of an aggressive exchange. It's a bad look if a big bouncer-type approaches someone in front of their friends without warning, and tells them to leave. If the person is embarrassed, you are guaranteed to get a barrage of insults and foul language which could escalate into fisticuffs.

192

Sid said that he always escorted punters out of a nightclub with commands and a polite explanation of why they were leaving against their will. But you'll get those who'll argue with you. And then they can get nasty and bring their friends in. That's when you'd be talking and gripping harder, getting the person outside as soon as possible, and sending them on their way. But there'll be those who'll come back at you. Arguing, abusing, carrying on like spoilt brats, and that's when you might have to ask them in what direction they live. But you're not supposed to. But the area's a grey one. The police don't want to get involved.

They've got better things to do. And they know how tough the floor man job is. You get to know a lot of the police. There's always mutual respect when you have a normal chat with them about the perils of night work. Sometimes, when things do get out of hand, when there's like an all-in brawl, which you can't handle, then the police have to be called in.

Sid gave Frank the name of a contact in Kings Cross in case he is interested. The person runs a number of nightclubs and strip joints and he's always looking for good men who can handle themselves in tough situations. He pays well but he expects high standards. Sid worked for him for five years, and he was respected for his work. A recommendation from him will go a long way in securing Frank a job.

Frank didn't say much during the conversation, but at the end of it he shook Sid's hand, and smiled, the first time he's smiled at a human since his early seminary days. He has smiled since, but only at animals and birds. Sid recognised the smile as an affirmation, and wished Frank good luck. They will never see each other again.

Canon 26 - When by the Rout he had made that Hideous Roar

The Demon's chorus:
THERE AT MIDNIGHT FRANK ENTERS HIS OWN,
HE IS RESPECTABLE AND HAS STREET CRED,
INTO THE DEVIL'S PLAYGROUND HE IS THROWN,
FOR PEDOPHILE PRIESTS THIS IS HIS LAIR.

Frank's contact was Abe Saffron. But before he went to meet him, Frank swapped his belongings at various op shops for a bowler hat, a long tapering black coat, high collar black shirts, black lapel trousers, black brogue shoes, a black belt, and finally a holstered whip.

Frank found a nearby park when he could sleep and after several days of speaking to various wary doormen about getting a job, one said he'd get back to him. But how could he be contacted? Frank told him he'd come by the same time each night. After two weeks Mr Saffron agreed to meet Frank at one of his establishments. As soon as he set eyes on Frank a strange feeling came over him. There was something about Frank which disturbed him. Something terrible and apocalyptic. A pensive Mr Saffron sat Frank down and read Sid's letter of recommendation. Then without hesitation Frank was offered a job as well as somewhere to sleep.

And before long Frank was working most nights at Saffron's night clubs and strip joints. To the punters he seemed aloof but when approached he spoke in a gentle voice. He was not there to judge, only to facilitate. He looked as though he could and would bounce anyone whom he deemed unfit to enter the door. And when working inside his gaze was enough. Though he was muscular, he was not as big as some of the other bouncers who were clearly ex wrestlers and the like. His chosen dress, although old fashioned, also garnered him respect. Mr. Saffron was pleased with Frank. The work had no tenure, but before long Frank was offered a contract.

194

With bluffing confidence, Frank had begun his work as a doorman. His presence was becoming somewhat hallowed, for in fact the punters were implicitly asking him that that they themselves might also be like him. But as they are clothed in provocative wear, they cannot cease to have a good time, and to let themselves go. When they return home, tired and a little more worn down, they will return to Frank like prodigal children and, as in a confessional or a court of law, recognize that they are reckless before him. Their hope is that they might have some redemption, the forgiveness of themselves, for they are still so young.

What might be also daunting to these young punters is that their unspoken outpouring of grief does not yet reinvigorate their hearts enough for them to forgive themselves. Self love, like the sea, is indivisible; they will love themselves when they comprehend how others love them. But as an individual all things are possible, as it is for Frank who, in his role as bouncer, forgives those who would trespass against him.

It is impossible for punters to follow the rules at the door by imitating each other at the outside; there is a vital participation, coming from the depths of common sense, in the manner of how punters proceed through the line, and then through the club's doorway, and on the floor, in seats and at the bar, watching, talking, dancing, laughing, until the early morning is drawn forth for bleary eyes to see, and no heart has spoken of aggression.

Frank's doorman respect is respect which is working to an end. It is not in Frank's demeanour to feel or to forget an offense against his work. His doorman experiences turned physical and verbally injurious sets forth leniency, which sanctifies his purpose, transforming absorbed hurt into gentle but firm intercession. None owe anything to Frank, instead they owe it to their leftover dignity which they need carry to their beds.

After some time in the job Frank thinks that there might be an advantage to the nature of the doorman role if he were named as though a character, like the Christ has become known for. Mr Saffron has already spoken to him regarding a character name. It might be necessary for punters to know the genus of his background, in order for them to respect him better. Even the most ordinary soldier in the Australian Regular Army has a character name of his own. Frank never had a nick name or an endearing name when he was young. It was always Frank, though occasionally it was dear Frank when his parents wanted something from him. Perhaps Frank, after he has earned his fame, will then become his character name. His demons will then tempt him into exploiting it for all the public to see, and he will fight them.

The punters need not have names for there is the herd in each of them. But when they are in trouble a name might be needed. Frank should distinguish an individual in the herd from the herd itself. He could well do so by asking the person's name. A character name shouldn't make Frank any less strange to the punters. It will designate him as one who is both mysterious and commanding. He will keep secret his values created in the Blue Mountains bush; those which had swept aside the errant Catholic ones. There is a controlled menace in him, for he has learnt to never trust professed truth, and a character name would be a bridge between he as a solitary person, and those in the herd who are the most trouble. And when his shift is finished and he takes off his long coat and bowler hat, so will his character name come off. It does not adhere to him when asleep or when he is aroused by a passion for or inspired by nature. And when he is pronounced by his bouncer kin over such time, for Frank is very good, it will be that his character name is spoken of in a jaw-breaking melodious tone, such that even Mr Saffron will privately sing of his praises.

And when the Horned Bouncer, as was now his character name, occasionally encounters the Bad Clergy, his feelings for them, for they are like brethren still, are a mixture of pity and contempt. They are lonely men trapped in an artificial crib. They cannot leave because they have nowhere normal to go. And as for the goosey two, he is getting close to sniffing them out and when he joins them in their darkness, having slipped on the Keeper's ring, that is when he will kill them.

www.ingramcontent.com/pod-product-compliance
Lightning Source LLC
Chambersburg PA
CBHW030427120726
47903CB00003B/842